Echoes of the Moon

by

Jennifer Taylor

Rhythm of the Moon Series

Echoes of the Moon

Cover Art by *Debbie Taylor*

The Wild Rose Press, Inc.
PO Box 708
Adams Basin, NY 14410-0708
Visit us at www.thewildrosepress.com

Publishing History
First Tea Rose Edition, 2017
Print ISBN 978-1-5092-1760-1
Digital ISBN 978-1-5092-1761-8

Rhythm of the Moon Series
Published in the United States of America

Through the buzzing in her ears,
a voice called to her from far away, low and resonant.

Strong arms cradled her, naked, and so warm. Her head lay against his chest, the hairs upon it tickling her ear. The muscles of his broad chest were hard and solid against her side, and so reassuring, rising and falling against her, encouraging her to suck in breath. But it was as if she sucked through a hollow reed.

"Bethan, you will be well soon. I'll take care of you."

He smelled of soap and earth. She clasped her arms tighter around his solid neck and closed her eyes. She'd not been held like this since childhood. He began to walk, carrying her as if she weighed no more than a kitten. Heat radiated from his chest, and his stomach muscles shifted and tensed as he headed toward the cottage.

She wheezed, then coughed.

"Don't worry, Bethan. I know what to do."

She nodded, her cheek rubbing against his chest, the curls there soft, yet pleasantly rough. His heart beat a reassuring rhythm against the uneven frantic beat of her heart.

"Georgie has the same problem. I've some herbs will help you. George!" he yelled. "Is there water left in the pot?"

"Aye, Da. What's wrong with Mistress Bethan?"

"She's having trouble breathing, much like you do."

"Da always makes me feel better, Mistress Bethan."

Protected. Safe.

Dedications

To Wayne:
You have my endless love and devotion.
There could be only you.
~*~

To my big sister, Suzanne:
Your big heart, loyalty, humor, and most of all,
love have saved me more than once. Thank you.
"Feelings strong, words difficult."
~*~

To my beloved mother Gloria,
who taught me the meaning of kindness and grace.

Chapter One

King's Harbour, England 1736

Bethan Owen stood in the doorway of the Siren Inn, drawing dawn's gray light around her like a cloak. She peered down the cobbled street at the English Channel, cool mist bathing her face and washing the sleep from her eyes. Patches of green churning sea sliced through the heavy fog, revealing a ribbon of pink and violet at the horizon. Her twin sister Elunid would be relieved when she awoke to see the sun in the sky, for every night at sunset she feared it would never return.

She sighed. If only her sister could break through the darkness like the sun. She straightened her shoulders, breathed in the fresh new day. She would draw strength from this moment of peace, for Elunid would require her utmost vigilance, and soon the inn would be bustling with customers. Who knew what new faces the tide would bring?

The squeak of wagon wheels on the next street over interrupted her reverie. Of course, who else would be working this time of day but Henry the night soil man and his son, George? Henry's bass voice rumbled softly, making her ears tingle. Why did the accursed man have such an effect on her?

"The tide rolls in, the tide rolls out

And brings adventure with it.
Be it rowboat or frigate, or schooner
They've stories to tell, fine items to sell
And I wish they'd be getting here sooner."

George joined in with his sweet tenor at a much higher volume.

"Too loud, Son. We mustn't disturb the good people of King's Harbour. They would not appreciate being awakened by the sound of their own shite hitting the barrel."

George giggled. "Da!"

Henry laughed, and every bit of skin on Bethan's body warmed in the cool air.

"Take a care, my boy. Lift with your legs. That's right. Climb up now, you may take the reins. Do you know where to go next?"

"Yes, Da."

She should go inside, have a peaceful cup of tea before Elunid awoke. Would her sister be defiant and fearful today? Or would she be like her old self, clever and funny with an intense artistic flair?

Instead she closed her eyes and leaned against the doorway, letting the man's soft, yet curiously cultured words glide into her, unraveling the worry tangling her thoughts like fishing rope.

"That's it. Easy there. You'll get more from this fine lady horse with a firm but gentle touch."

Like Henry's touch upon her arm, mindful of her safety as they'd searched for Elunid a few months ago. A most noxious odor wafted up the street, quashing the memory of his touch. The wagon appeared around the corner at the bottom of the street, and the two hopped out.

Henry grunted as they lifted the yoke into their shoulders, the barrel at the end. "Remember what the old bard said?"

"I don't know. He said a lot of things."

"Oh, it is excellent to have a giant's strength, but it is tyrannous to use it like a giant."

Bethan forgot the stench upon recognizing the words of William Shakespeare. *Measure for Measure?* How did a night soil man come to quote the immortal words of the bard? Most puzzling, and likely the reason she couldn't get Henry out of her mind.

They soon returned to the wagon, and Henry watched George, a small smile on his face.

George scratched the horse behind the ears. "Good girl. I shall never hurt you."

They made their way up the street, and the closer they got, the more repulsive the odor became. She covered her mouth with a handkerchief but couldn't take her eyes away from his broad shoulders and wide back, looking strong enough to carry any burden. Even hers. He waved at her and strode up the street.

He walks like royalty, not as if he has the most disgusting job in town. She lowered the cloth as curiosity got the better of her.

He stopped a good twenty paces from her, took off his work gloves, and bowed. "I shan't get too close, Mistress Bethan. Good morrow." He had eyes the color of Lena's best summer ale. "You're up early."

She nodded. "It's peaceful this time of day, when the town is still asleep."

"Except for us." He grinned. He wore no hat, and his black hair curled around his face. "I enjoy my work for the same reason."

"You enjoy your work?" Was the man mad?

He nodded, his eyes darkening from summer ale to stout. "Why should I not, despite the nature of it? It's honest and important work." He turned toward his son. "And a good trade for young George to learn."

What a snob she was. "I didn't mean to insult."

He stepped forward, and she stepped back, rapping her elbow on the door frame. "Ouch!"

He rushed toward her. "Are you all right?"

His fingers on her arm were warm and reassuring as she closed her eyes and waited for the stars to disappear from her vision. Then she came to her senses and recoiled from him.

He backed away. "I'm sorry to have disturbed your reverie, Mistress Bethan." Formal, cold.

Emptiness echoed in the pit of her stomach; she had offended him. Why should she care? Nevertheless, she watched him retreat down the hill toward his son. Such a mystery. She jumped at the touch of a slender hand on her shoulder.

"What are you looking at, *Chwaer*?"

She turned to Elunid. On days when her twin was lucid, it was like looking at herself in a mirror: dark blue eyes, winged brows below a widow's peak, brown hair threaded with black.

"Ellie, what have you got all over yourself?"

Pale brown bits of *something* lay on her twin's haphazardly tied apron, all the way up her crookedly laced bodice. They lay on her neck and bosom like bits of wheat against a snow-covered pasture.

"Even on your face!" Bethan lifted the corner of her neat apron and wiped Elunid's face.

Her twin stood stock still during her ministrations.

4

She watched the night man and his son work their way up the street. "Ah."

It appeared Elunid would be lucid today, at least for now.

"What do you mean?" Bethan asked.

Elunid turned and met her gaze. "Yon shite gatherer. You fancy him; deny it not, Sister."

"I do not fancy him. How could I possibly?"

"The better question is why would you not? Look at the way his haunches move as he walks. He would be the perfect model for Hephaestus, god of fire."

Breathing slowly sometimes assisted Bethan with well-needed patience. "Come now, Elunid!"

She waggled her winged brows. "Are *you* on fire, Bethan?"

Her face grew warm. "I am not!"

Lena, the alewife and owner of the Siren Inn appeared, huffing and red-faced. With a work-worn hand, she shoved her white blonde hair out of her face. "*Ach*, there you are. I can't turn my back for one minute."

"What happened, Lena?" The moment Bethan feared had likely come to pass: Lena had decided they were too much of a burden.

Lena put her arm around Elunid, but she shrugged against the alewife's touch.

"No, *Liebchen*, you will come with me." Lena turned to Bethan. "I had her drying mugs, and she wandered off. Next thing I knew, she had her hands in the wort. Thank God it had cooled."

Part of the beer-making process involved the boiling of hops and other grains. It was a grueling and sometimes dangerous endeavor. But it smelled wonderful.

"Elunid, why ever would you stick your hand in a pot of wort? We're lucky you didn't scald yourself."

Elunid started and picked a bit of wheat off her bodice. She held it in front of her, turning it about in her hands. "It is the perfect color for the cross."

"The cross?"

The corners of her mouth creased with irritation. She spoke slowly, as if to a simpleton. "The cross in the needlework the Holy Ones have commissioned—no—demanded I do for them. I cannot find the right color."

"I'll take you to buy thread later," Bethan said.

Lena shook her head. "Bethan, what are you two doing out here so early?" She guided them in and shut the heavy door.

Elunid hummed a strange melancholy tune, raising the hairs on the back of Bethan's neck.

"Poor child," the alewife whispered.

"I'm sorry, Lena. You'll soon grow tired of us, I fear."

Lena clasped Bethan's hands. "You're freezing. And see you don't worry about staying here. For I could not do without your help with the baby, the running of the inn, your..." She wiped a tear from her cheek. "Your friendship."

Lena was prone to melancholy since the brutal death of her beloved husband Josef six months ago.

"Thank you, Lena. Why don't you rest a bit?"

She sank into the chair. "I'll put up my feet for just a moment, then I must get back to the wort before little Josef wakes up. I've made oyster stew and bread. You two are thin as waifs."

She made to rise, but Bethan put a hand on her

shoulder. "No, you rest. I'll get it."

"This is why I cannot do without you." She sighed. "You spoil me."

Bethan smiled as she fetched the bowls of stew and some freshly baked bread and set the meal before them. She wasted no time tucking into her own. How fortunate she and Elunid were; Lena's excellent food made a person feel warm with the comfort of it.

Of course Elunid hadn't touched hers. She obviously hadn't slept well, with those half-moons of gray under her eyes, skin pale as moonflowers. Bethan put the spoon in her hand, put it to her mouth. "You must eat."

"Will she not even eat the warm bread?"

Elunid opened her mouth, took two bites, and stared fixedly at the bowl. The bread lay untouched.

Bethan shook her head. "Only on rare occasions, for she thinks it is the Holy Communion, and it would be sacrilege to do so."

"Can nothing be done for the poor girl?"

If there was, she didn't know what it was. God knows she'd tried to find help for her. She picked up her spoon again. The stew caressed Bethan's tongue with creaminess, and chunks of oyster burst a salty sea flavor into her mouth. How good to partake of something so delicious and forget the troubles of everyday life. She dunked the remainder of her bread in the cream and sighed with pleasure. "Lena, you must show me how to make this. It's heaven."

At the word, "heaven," her twin's head popped up, and she dropped the spoon. It clattered into the bowl and splashed soup on her bodice. "My work is not worthy for the angels yet. I'm not ready." She stood and ripped the cap off her head.

"Sister, sit down. I was only talking about the soup, how delicious it was."

Elunid sat back down, wary.

"Will you not eat a bit more?"

Elunid closed her eyes. "Eat equals fat, fat equals lazy, lazy cannot do the work for the Holy Ones."

Lena gasped.

"Excellent," Bethan said. "All the more for me then."

With the keen hearing all mothers seem to possess, Lena tilted her head and listened. "Ah. The baby's awake." With a grunt she rose and hurried into her private apartment.

After finishing the last of the soup, Bethan filled the teapot with hot water from the ever-present pot of water hanging over the fire. She brought the teapot to the table, put the tea in it. Elunid watched with rapt attention as the tea steeped. She soon handed Elunid a cup. "There you go. Just the way you like it."

Bethan had just settled down with her tea when a customer walked in. She rose, keeping one eye on Elunid.

The customer, a tall, well-built lad of around twenty, swept off a black slouch hat to reveal carrot red hair and a freckled face. He grinned. "Good morn to ye, mistress."

Bethan nodded. "Good morning. What can I do for you?"

His blue eyes scanned her body up and down. "So many ways I could reply, lovey."

She grimaced. Seemed like such a wholesome lad until he opened his mouth. "There's oyster stew ready, and fresh bread right out of the oven."

"Smells as delicious as you look." He winked. "The name's Freddy."

Best to ignore his forwardness.

He flashed the same grin at Elunid, who didn't bother to look up. She'd opened the teapot and spooned the tea leaves onto a linen napkin. Separating them with a spoon, she lined them up according to light and dark.

He stepped backward, eyes wide. "How is it I'm blessed with the beauty of not just one, but two? You are doubles."

"Yes." Bethan folded her arms. "Do you want to eat?"

In the few short months they'd been at Lena's, she'd grown accustomed to dealing with the likes of this lad. When they'd lived at the lighthouse, she'd have been shocked at his behavior. Now it was just part of everyday life, and preferable to the isolation of the lighthouse, with only Mother and Elunid for company.

Seemingly unfazed by her stern manner, he grinned. "Some stew and bread sound just the thing, with your summer ale."

"I'll be back." She glanced at Elunid, who was still occupied at her task. She hustled into the kitchen, ladled the stew into a bowl, and cut a generous slice of bread.

She returned to find the red-haired lad sitting next to Elunid, one freckled and filthy hand upon her arm.

"What are you doing there, love?" He picked up bits of tea and disordered them.

Elunid stiffened and shoved him away. "Now, see what you've done."

Caught unawares, he tumbled off his chair.

9

Elunid stood and towered over him, fists clenched. "Begone, shit wit."

He stood and put his filthy clothes to rights. "Foul mouthed trollop."

Bethan strode over to him and held the tray over his head. Sometimes being "freakishly tall," as her mother said, came in handy. "I'll thank you to keep away from my sister."

She jerked her head in the direction of the table in the far corner. He skulked away, cringing just a tad when she brought his food over. "I meant no harm."

She walked off without a word. As she busied herself washing glasses, she kept her eye on him. Something about him set her nerves on edge. And did he think she didn't see the speculative glances he gave Elunid?

She let out a little puff of relief when he put his money on the table.

He grinned. "Thank ye, miss. Set me to rights, it did."

When she didn't respond to his "charm," he glanced from one twin to the other. "'Twasn't only the food set me to rights. Seeing two such beautiful doubles as…"

Elunid hissed. "Why are you still here?"

He flung his hands up in mock alarm. "Why such venom?"

"You."

"Do you own the place?"

"No."

"Does the owner know how welcome you make the guests, sweeting?"

The dark edge to his voice further confirmed

Elunid's uncanny instinct for sniffing out ne'er-do-wells.

Bethan didn't respond, but stood as tall as her height allowed, and glared toward the door.

He bowed clumsily, set his hat upon his head, and whistled himself out the door.

Elunid stared at the door, a fine tremor taking hold.

At that moment, Lena walked in with the babe balanced on her hip. "What's amiss?"

"Nothing we can't handle."

Bethan shook off the ill wind that swept over her.

Chapter Two

Henry's shoulder muscles strained with fatigue as he and George lifted the pole to their shoulders and carried their night's load to where the farmer pointed.

"We've got your gold, Zeke."

The old man took his pipe from his wizened lips. "Are ye a smuggler now, young Henry?"

They carefully set the bucket down and spread the material, backing away quickly once the deed was done.

Henry laughed. "If I'm a smuggler, none but the likes of you would want my treasure."

"Har. True enough. From the looks of it, the town's eating well."

"Yes, and thanks to you and your fine harvest of potatoes, the ladies are plump and sumptuous." Who could blame him if he resorted to a little earthy humor from time to time?

"Good to hear. I don't see so well these days, but I could feel my way." Zeke laughed. "I'll bring turnips and potatoes your way this afternoon." He squinted at George, who sat on the ground petting his sheepdog. "Gotten tall, he has."

George gave the dog's head a final pat and jumped to his feet. "I'm hungry, Da."

"I expect you are, lad. We'll fry up some ham with eggs and the Wilson's good bread." He waved to the farmer, and they were on their way.

"Do we have any more jam?"

"No, but we'll get some in town after we get a little rest. I promised I'd give Mistress Lena a hand tonight. There's a ship full of sailors coming in."

"I love to go to town during the day! Mistress Lena always feeds me, and Bethan is so kind."

Henry smiled. "She is." If only she'd award him with the same attention she gave George.

George clucked his tongue to hasten the horse on their short journey to the cottage.

"Now you may sing as loud as you like, my lad."

The promise of stripping off the soiled work clothes, refreshment, a good meal, and most of all, George's sweet tenor soaring through the air was their favorite part of the day.

"How about 'My One-Eyed Lass'?"

"Whatever pleases you."

The rumble of the wheels provided the rhythm to the boy's song, with Henry's bass joining in. They soon arrived at their thicket of trees and parked the wagon at the far end of the property.

"Set the horse free, and don't forget to brush her down. Then we must wash."

"But I'm so hungry."

"As am I. What do we do every morning after work?"

"We wash," George mumbled.

"Yes. For just because we're night soil men doesn't mean we must reek of it."

George quickened his pace, and they gathered at the water's edge on their property. It had been a pleasant surprise indeed when Henry discovered the mineral springs. They stripped off their clothing in the cool air. Steam rose from the water, and Henry sighed as he slipped into its warmth. George followed suit with a splash and a whoop.

The hot, sulphurous water soaked into Henry's aching muscles, melting the night's work away. He closed his eyes, and Bethan's tall, proud body appeared, fresh as dawn's first breeze. Her dark brows rose when he approached her and took her hand. Would the delicate pale skin on her long neck turn rosy when she joined him in the water? Would her eyes darken with the bliss of it?

A heavy hand on his head dunking him under the water interrupted his reverie. He emerged, spluttering. "George!"

The boy laughed, joyful as a basket of puppies. "I got you this time."

"Yes, you did, you little heathen!"

"I'm getting stronger, like Hercules."

"To be sure, George. But if you want to eat, you will wash from top to bottom as you must do every day. Here's the soap, and mind you don't miss a spot. Don't forget your hair. As long as we have coin for soap, we'll not go about town reeking."

He lifted the boy and threw him into the air as high as he could, closing his eyes against the splash. He kept an eye on George's washing and indulged in his reverie about the tall, dark-haired beauty. He should be realistic and attend one of the country dances again, meet a simple girl who wouldn't recoil from his touch like Bethan, because of his lowly job. It was how he'd met his second wife, who'd died of smallpox a few years ago, God rest her soul. She'd been a good woman, a kind stepmother to George. He shouldn't ask for more than that. But Bethan...

The way her eyes widened with curiosity when he'd quoted Shakespeare, leaving him no choice but to climb into their depths. She could not puzzle him out. He would encourage her curiosity, endeavor to make her eyes glitter.

He scrubbed his face with his palms. Why would he continue to torture himself so, when he needed to concentrate on making a life for his boy among the people of the town who'd welcomed them five years ago with open arms? Not like his own family. He glanced over at George, who floated on his back, eyes open to the clear summer sky. He would not poison the beauty of the day with thoughts of them. The two of them, he and George, must be enough.

Before long, they broke their fast on the worn trestle table with a fire in the fireplace. Henry let the boy take the edge off his hunger before correcting his manners.

"Don't slurp your tea, George. And try not to hold your fork as if you're holding a shovel."

"I hold a shovel most nights."

"But some day you might want to court a young lady and take her for tea."

"Aw, no! Why would I do that?"

Henry chuckled. "Are we not going to tea at the Shipwreck Hotel for your birthday?"

George nodded.

"Yes, and every man needs to know how to conduct himself in society. Even men with lowly jobs, in my humble opinion."

"Why, Da?"

"Because sometimes life takes us to places we never expected to go."

George nodded and stuffed another piece of ham into his mouth. Had he eaten so much as a boy? Perhaps when Mother wasn't looking.

"Are you going to read *One Thousand and One Nights* before we sleep?"

"Are you not tired, George?"

"Yes, but I love a story before bed. It makes me dream of grand things." He'd a bit of egg on his chin.

Henry brought his napkin to his own mouth, and as he thought he would, George imitated him.

"I'm remembering to wipe my mouth, see?"

"Well done, boy. Do you like the story?"

"Oh yes. Very much. S'my favorite so far."

"Now, I must warn you: we will practice your letters before we go into town."

Many would deem it fruitless and even cruel to make George practice his letters. Certainly his family had given up on teaching him before they'd even begun. But he would give his boy the same chance as others at learning how to read. He kept the lessons short, and over the course of a few years, he had learned the alphabet to the letter "m." He would not give up on his George.

"I remember reading it to your mother. She enjoyed it too, but not the parts with the fighting."

"The fighting's my favorite part."

"I quite agree, Georgie. More tea?"

He shook his head. "What was she like?"

Henry closed his eyes in memory. "She was giving and sweet. Never said a cruel word to anyone."

The morning after George's birth, Celia lay

propped with pillows, very pale, but glowing. She held a squalling George in her arms, and they reveled in the sound as they bent their heads over him. Then, later that night, as he eased himself into bed after a celebratory glass of port, he found her in a pool of blood. Neither the midwife or the doctor could stop the bleeding.

He forced himself to focus on George's face, the living blessing of their love. "She loved to put her hand in a pile of dirt, to plant a seed. She grew the biggest cucumbers and brightest roses in the county. The smell of roses always reminds me of her."

"She sounds grand."

"She was. And though she only got a day with you, she loved you very much."

He would give up anything to protect his son's heart, even from the people who were supposed to love him the most.

Chapter Three

Later that afternoon, Bethan and Elunid made their way down the cobbles of Siren Street to Maggie Pierce's house. Bethan felt a surge of excitement at the prospect of what she might learn from the knowledgeable midwife. As they skirted the harbor, she took heart in the sight of the English Channel, waves rising toward the summer sun. A day so warm and bright—she could sing with the joy of it. Who would the sea bring to her today?

Elunid poked her in the arm. "Thinking of yon shite master?"

The ocean could take a lesson from Elunid's unpredictability. Not even Bethan could see into her depths. Certainly not their mother, who'd taken to her bed and sent them to their older sister, Polly. But it didn't take long for her twin's behavior to frighten the children. Thank God Lena had taken them in.

A fishing boat bobbed in the water, resounding with singing and laughter. Two men stood above a net full of fish. A flock of gulls took turns swooping for the guts. The view was so clear Bethan could make out a man's homespun breeches and his spyglass aimed toward shore.

He pointed at the two women. "Take a look, Roy. I'm seeing double, and I'm not even drinking yet."

The man grabbed the spyglass. "Two such beauties

will surely be in my dreams, or better yet my lap, tonight."

"Oh, to be sure. You're too cowardly to even speak to a woman, unless you're asking her how much."

"Gets the job done."

Bethan grimaced and quickened her pace. "Come along, Sister."

She came to an abrupt halt upon realizing she walked alone. She turned.

Elunid bent over the cobbles, a beetle in her hand. "Look." She held it up. "Note the cobalt blue, the shade of green, shiny black, black, shiny silk, Sister. Cobalt blue, the color of Peter's eyes."

"Peter?"

She squeezed Bethan's arm. "The fisherman."

Fisherman? Who could she have met without her knowledge? "What?"

"Lack-a-wit!" Her eyebrows creased in irritation. She peered into Bethan's face. "Christ. Peter. Fish."

Oh. The Bible. "No need to take that tone with me."

Elunid squeezed her arm again. "Peter. Beetle prophet, ocean scholar, time-tuning imbecile." She shook her head, disgust coarsening the smooth complexion.

Bethan swallowed hard. This didn't bode well; the word nonsense often meant a harbinger of worse behavior to come. Perhaps Ian the apothecary had something to calm her. He was forever searching for remedies for conditions of the mind.

They turned onto Market Street and soon arrived at Maggie and Ian's shoppe.

"I must speak with Maggie. She wanted me to pay

her a visit this morning."

"Carry on then, Madame Lack-a-Wit."

Bethan stifled a laugh. Elunid's curses could be quite inventive.

They entered the shoppe to find Maggie sitting on Ian's lap, no easy feat due to her advanced pregnancy. Ian kissed her thoroughly, in such a way that made Bethan grow warm. So this was how it was done!

Maggie broke away. "I'm too heavy for you."

"No, you're not."

"This can't be good for your legs."

"I can't feel them. But I can feel this." He kissed her again, this time trailing the backs of his long fingers down the front of her bodice and over the swell of her belly. "Bounteous and beloved," he murmured.

"Ahem." Bethan cleared her throat.

Maggie started and stood, her face red. "Oh. Good afternoon."

In an admirable economy of movement, Maggie pulled her ebony hair up and pinned it under a cap.

Ian grinned. "Could my afternoon be any grander? Greetings, ladies."

Elunid knitted her brows at him, but her lips twitched. Even Elunid was not totally immune to Ian's charm.

He sat rather sprawled on the chair and proceeded to pull each leg up with his arms, to straighten himself. "There we go."

His green eyes gleamed like pirate's treasure. He glanced between the two girls, then focused his bright gaze upon Elunid. "Mistress Elunid. Is your needlework progressing as it should?"

His look of compassion brought tears to Bethan's

eyes. Scarcely anyone made the effort to understand Elunid's mind, inasmuch as one could. But Ian was different, having an affliction of his own, beyond his physical challenge.

"Have you found what you need to fulfill your purpose?"

Elunid stood still, then her face lit up with a smile that transformed her. Her sister really was quite beautiful when she smiled.

"The man could charm the skin off a kipper," Maggie said.

"I sense an upcoming storm." Bethan glanced at the shelves of herbs and medicine and met Ian's gaze. Ian understood immediately and nodded.

He lifted himself from the chair, upper arms bulging with muscle, grasped the counter, and worked his way behind. He stood for a moment with his head down. Then he lifted his gaze and grinned. "Tell me more about your endeavor, Elunid. I know how important it is to you."

Elunid came to the counter, and Maggie motioned for Bethan to follow her in the parlor. "I need a word with you."

Bethan stood for a moment, breathing in the intoxicating smell of fresh roses. A huge bouquet of pink and red tea roses stood on the table in the center of the small but cozy room. "What lovely roses."

Maggie bent over the flowers and buried her face in the blooms. When she emerged, she seemed to wear the color on her face. "Though Ian cannot gather the flowers himself, a young dogs body does it for him. I tell him there's no need to court me with these ridiculous love tokens, but he never listens."

Bethan smiled. What must it be like to glow with the love of someone? No sense in speculating on what would never be.

"Bethan, I think I may deliver this child sooner than expected. Are you ready to become the town's midwife?"

"I hope so. I think so."

"Two women are due to deliver before me. One of them has had a baby before, one has not. I must be honest with you."

"Please do so."

"I've not known you long, and you're very young."

"I don't feel young."

"The care of your sister has required much from you, and I know you've not had an easy life. But you are a virgin, are you not?"

Her face burned. "Of course."

"You're innocent of the ways of the flesh, the inner privities of a woman and the man's invasion of them required to make a babe."

"Does it matter?"

"I don't believe so. But others will."

Bethan shrugged. "It doesn't matter what people think. Assisting you with the birth of Polly's twins was the most exhilarating, terrifying thing I've ever done. And the most joyful. I can be a blessing to the women of this town." In a way she never could for her sister.

"You have much to learn."

Bethan nodded. "I'll do whatever it takes, for the promise of new life excites me like nothing else."

"I truly don't know how long I have before the baby arrives. It could be a fortnight, could be a week, but I know my husband." She nodded her head in the direction of the shoppe counter. "He's been nagging me like an old crone already, and it will only get worse with every passing day."

"What about your sister Sarah? She'll be at the birthing, won't she?" Knowing another experienced midwife would be present would certainly be reassuring.

Maggie sank down into the rocking chair. "I'm afraid you cannot depend on my sister these days. Her behavior is…sometimes when we're talking, she gets a blank look on her face, as if she sees right through me. And what alarms me even more is her inability to hold a conversation. It seems her ordeal is always with her."

"The poor thing."

"Bethan, I cannot depend on my sister to see me through in my time of need."

"Maggie, I promise I will attend to you as if you were my own sister."

"You were a quick study at your sister's birth, and I know you will learn much still." She hefted herself out of the divan with an unladylike grunt. "Besides, the Holy Nun tells me to have faith in you, Bethan."

Before she could respond to Maggie's strange comment, Elunid giggled.

"Ian has a way with her."

"He has an affinity with people who suffer from afflictions of the mind."

They fell silent for a moment as Maggie gazed at her husband.

Maggie waddled over to the bookcase and pulled out a thick, battered book. She caressed the cover, handed it to Bethan with the reverence a priest would give his bible.

"It's heavy."

"Read the midwife manual whenever you get a spare moment. You'll learn much."

Just then, the door opened, and Ruthie, Maggie's niece, entered. "Aunt Maggie, Uncle Ian!"

"My beauty," Ian crowed. "So happy to see you."

Sarah's daughter skipped into the parlor and straight into Maggie's arms. She had inherited her father, Samuel's black hair and had the long gangly legs of a yearling.

"Auntie, you're very big."

She held her little hands over the midwife's belly with a professional air, bringing a smile to Maggie's face.

"How are you, my sweet? I've missed you. You must come over more."

Ruthie's shoulders slumped. "I've been helping Mother."

Maggie grasped her little hand. "How does she fare?"

A shadow passed over her face, making her look older than her years. "Not well. Not ill in her body but will not stir from her chair, staring at... I know not what." Her eyes filled with tears. "Father sent me to see if Uncle Ian had a—what did he call it?—stimulant?"

"Where's Gracie?"

"Sister's playing at Joanie's. She likes to be around her children."

Maggie nodded. "Don't worry, Ruthie. Your mother is going to be fine."

Ruthie bit her bottom lip. Poor child. She'd had to grow up quickly, after the trauma her mother had suffered two years ago. And no wonder Sarah was altered; how could anyone survive being buried alive without ill effects?

"Ruthie, go speak with Uncle Ian. He has some Turkish delight for you."

"Ooh!" And suddenly she transformed into a little girl again.

Bethan eyed Maggie's belly. How could something so immense come out of a woman's body? And she was responsible for her and the child's safety. Uneasiness crawled up her spine.

As if she sensed her doubt, Maggie said, "You have your sister to care for. Can you shoulder all the responsibility?"

She nodded.

"Mind you, I'll attend the births if I am able."

Ian's voice carried into the parlor. "Not if I have my say. She should go to bed with the chickens every night."

"I agree."

Maggie folded her arms and gave Bethan the gimlet eye. "Whose side are you on?"

Bethan grinned. "I'm on the side of the babe who needs a rested mother. We should be on our way."

"Goodbye," Ruthie called. "Father said I must come right back."

Maggie shook her head after they said their goodbyes. "Poor girl. Sit and have some tea. Rest while you can, for it's going to be a busy summer."

"It's you who should be resting." Bethan herded Maggie to the divan and put a stool under her feet. Was it normal for a woman's ankles and feet to swell?

She prepared tea and called Ian and Elunid in. Ian made his way slowly with the aid of a cane and plopped down in the chair, shaking from the effort and cursing under his breath.

Elunid leaned over Ian and gestured with her long arms while Ian dodged them in an exaggerated manner. "You see, the color of the cross is significant, and must be perfect."

Bethan sighed. "Elunid, have you tried a tea cake? They're delicious. Almonds."

One eyebrow rose. "Oh. Well then." She sat down, and Bethan handed her a cake, which she promptly put in her mouth. "Yes indeed. White and delightsome."

Maggie rested her teacup on her stomach, eyes intent on Elunid. Suddenly, the tea cup rattled, and her stomach rolled and bucked. "Ack!"

None of them could drag their eyes away, for it seemed as if the babe would burst right through her skin.

"Holy balls of shit!" Elunid gasped.

"Elunid!" She couldn't take her twin anywhere.

"A little earthy, but well put." Ian chuckled.

The door to the shoppe burst open.

"Hallo! Is anyone there?"

"Yes, Henry. We're in the parlor."

"Ian, we've a gift for you. But we have to get it through the door first."

Chapter Four

Bethan rushed into the shoppe room. George held the door open while Henry pushed a wooden chair with wheels upon it through the door.

"All right then, George. Let's see if we measured correctly."

Henry eased the chair through the doorway. "Oh, Bethan. Good afternoon."

His large, muscular hands caressed the handles of the strange chair. He could crush the wood if he wanted to. His eyes glowed like the polished wood.

George held his three-cornered hat to his chest and bowed. "Good afternoon, Mistress Bethan."

The two wore identical wide grins, and her heart knocked against her chest.

Henry joined Bethan in the background, grinning as George showed off the contraption.

"You made this?"

Henry nodded, brows raised. "Are you surprised a lowly night laborer could make such a thing of beauty?"

How did he always manage to make her feel uncharitable? "No, not at all. I've just never seen such a thing. It's a fine piece of furniture, actually."

Henry's grin lit his face, as if her praise meant something to him.

"We've been working on it since it seemed

apparent Ian would not walk for a while, or ever." He whispered the last two words.

"I helped polish it," George said.

"You're so skilled," Bethan said. "Why do you work all night gathering shite?" It popped out of her mouth before she could stop it.

He filled the room with his broad shoulders, making her feel shielded with his steady strength. She swallowed. "I meant you could be a carpenter instead, couldn't you?"

"Oh, I'm not a carpenter."

She ran her hands along the side of it and felt his gaze upon them. "It's quite intricate, which must involve a lot of planning and figuring."

"You think I've not the intellect for it?" He grinned. His eyes had changed from a warm brown to hazel, with flecks of blue and green. The scent of sandalwood and cedar tempted her to draw nearer.

"You twist my words, sir!"

"I'm sorry, Mistress Bethan."

"You don't *sound* sorry, Da."

"Don't be impertinent, George. You asked a very logical question, milady. And it's clear you can't help your curiosity any more than George here can help liking trifles."

"'Tis true." George nodded, hair flopping in his eyes.

"I will answer your question, at least in part. When it comes to carpentry, I only know what Josef taught me, God rest his soul." He bowed his head, and in perfect imitation, George did the same.

She giggled, then blushed. "Oh, I'm sorry."

Fortunately, Ian struggled in with the aid of a cane

and Maggie's assistance.

"Henry, my good fellow. What is that you have there?"

"Mr. Ian, look what Da and I made for you." George gestured grandly toward the chair in the middle of the room.

Ian and Maggie approached the chair, running their hands over the smooth wood.

"It's beautiful," Ian exclaimed.

"Look at the detail." Maggie pointed at the scrolled handles.

"Get in, Ian," Henry said. "Let's see how it fits."

Henry and George helped him into it, and Ian rested his long fingers on the wheels, experimenting with the movement, rolling it back and forth.

"Oh, it's grand! Henry, you are the finest friend a man could ever have. Thank you. I can never repay you."

"No need," Henry said gruffly. "And nothing you would not do for me, if I needed it."

Bethan's eyes filled with tears despite herself. The apothecary's joy was contagious as he bent forward and wheeled himself about, and Bethan could not help laughing as he bumped into the wall, eliciting cries of alarm from Maggie.

"Mayhap you need a pillow at your back."

"Don't coddle me, woman. It's very comfortable, as if it was custom made, which it was." He waggled his brows. "Sit upon my lap, my lovely. I'll give you a ride."

Henry lurched forward. "Uh, I'm not sure the chair can accommodate…"

"Someone as enormous as me?"

The midwife could look threatening when provoked. But just then, her belly heaved and an apparent elbow or a foot poked out from the bottom of her ribcage. She groaned.

"Ho, my offspring doesn't agree with your indignation." He wheeled over to her and took her hand. "Remember, you are not fat, you are with child, and even if you were the size of a clipper ship, it would just mean there is more of you to love, Queen Sumptuous."

Bethan glanced at Henry, who wore an odd look of amusement and—was it longing? While she could never hope for the possibility of someone who loved her with all their heart, why should he not hope for such a thing?

Where was Elunid? She must have slipped out during all the excitement. "Excuse me. I must go find my sister."

In her haste she ran into Henry's solid torso. He placed his hands upon her shoulders to steady her, and suddenly she couldn't breathe. So warm, his body radiating strength, but his fingers so gentle upon her, as if she were precious and rare.

"She's sitting in the parlor," he murmured, his breath brushing her cheeks like a kiss. Their lips were close enough they could have easily kissed. What did his lips feel like? She broke away.

In the parlor, Elunid sat with a piece of cloth, unravelling the embroidery.

"Ellie, no!" She snatched it from her hand. The material itself was of very fine silk and the artistry of the exotic bird magnificent.

"Don't disturb me. I have found the brown I need

for the cross in the tree branch upon which the bird sits. They are well pleased."

"Is anything amiss?" Maggie rushed in, holding her stomach.

"I'm so sorry, Maggie. She's fine, but your embroidery isn't."

Maggie shrugged. "Don't worry, Bethan. It's just a thing."

Ian had brought the rare embroidered cloth back from his travels. When a man selects a gift for the woman he loves, it is a precious thing. Or so she'd heard. "I know it had sentimental value." She handed it to Maggie.

Maggie put her hand on Bethan's arm. "Don't fret about it, Bethan."

Elunid loomed over Bethan and poked her in the chest. "I told you I need thread, woman."

"Enough, Sister."

"Here, Elunid." Maggie handed the cloth to her. "With my blessing. I'll look forward to seeing what you're making."

"It's not for your eyes," Elunid mumbled.

Bethan took her sister by the arm. How nice for her to never have to be responsible for her own behavior. "Thank you, Maggie, and I'm so sorry."

Maggie smiled. "We'll speak soon, Bethan."

Elunid headed for the door. Bethan had no time to give her regards to the men, who celebrated Ian's new acquisition with a glass of sherry. As she opened the door, the hairs on the back of her neck stood up as she felt Henry's gaze upon her.

As they walked, Bethan decided to make a foray into manners, however fruitless.

"Elunid, must you be so rude? It was bad enough, destroying Maggie's cloth, but not to apologize or express gratitude for her generosity. Two words: sorry and thank you." Had she not spent half her life apologizing for her?

Elunid fingered the linen and met Bethan's gaze. "Do you not understand? Much is required of me, and my life is not my own."

Bethan decided not to comment and followed her into the store. She must have a plan to have Elunid supervised when she delivered babies. Lena, who already had her hands full? Or Sabine, Lena's adopted daughter? George had a soothing effect on her, but he was too young for such a responsibility.

As Elunid perused the thread supply for what seemed like hours, Bethan let her mind drift to the time before her sister's illness. Even during their idyllic early childhood by the sea, their mother was often abed, but the two of them played on the beach with Davyd, the local gentry's son.

She and Elunid created stories on the sand, and Bethan would sing to the sea, mouth wide open, the music carrying on the wind. Davyd was their captive audience.

Ellie always found ways of coloring the sand. She created intricate artwork and cried like a babe when the water carried it away.

Their hoyden lifestyle ended when their father went to sea and never returned, and they moved into the lighthouse.

After she paid for Elunid's purchases, they followed the delicious aroma wafting from the Wilson's bake shoppe.

Elunid sniffed. "Cinnamon buns." She walked toward the shoppe.

"Excellent idea."

Mrs. Wilson slathered icing on a tray of buns still warm from the oven. "Well, here I thought my eyes were giving me fits, to see the two of you, so alike."

"It must be our mutual love for your wonderful baking." Really, there was nothing better.

"Please, girls. Let me fetch you plates, and you can sit and chat with me awhile." She glanced at her daughter Isadora and whispered behind her hand. "What with Mistress Woebegone there."

Isadora stood behind the counter. Mayhap they could be friends, for there weren't many women their age in town.

Isadora nodded curtly and began transferring loaves of bread into the display case.

"For heaven's sake, girl," Mrs. Wilson snapped. "Have you no manners? Greet your neighbors."

Bethan laid a hand on Mrs. Wilson's arm. "It's fine. Sometimes I'm of the same mood."

"No excuse for bad manners."

Isadora sighed and approached them. "Good morning." She lowered her eyes, which were a brilliant blue. Her neck and face were riddled with pockmarks, but she had a shapely figure and a graceful way about her when she wasn't pouting.

"It's lovely to see you, Isadora. You must come round the inn and have a cup of tea with Elunid and me."

"I…" Isadora stared at Elunid, who gobbled the cinnamon roll as if she'd not eaten for days.

Mrs. Wilson crowed. "Now, there's a girl with an

appetite. I can't abide a girl who won't eat for vanity's sake." Her philosophy was reflected in her robust figure, and who could blame her? She handed Elunid another one.

Elunid licked the icing of the bun slowly. "White as a disciple."

Mother and daughter turned their heads in her direction.

"Your cinnamon buns are her very favorite treat." Bethan popped the last bite into her mouth.

She turned to Isadora. "I imagine you're missing your own sister. Have you heard from Bess?"

Isadora set her mouth in a thin line. "Her new husband is perfect. Her house is perfect. Her life is perfect, while I'm here toiling away."

"Isadora." Mrs. Wilson strode over and grabbed her by the chin. "There's no one on God's earth whose life is perfect, your sister included. No one likes a sulker, and it does nothing for your looks, to be sure."

Bethan cringed in sympathy for the girl.

"Sorry, Mother."

"Isadora," Bethan touched her arm. "Would you like to walk back to the inn with us?" She glanced at Martha. "If you can spare her, of course."

"No thank you." She avoided Bethan's eyes. "I have someplace I must go." Without another word, she walked out the door.

Martha shook her head. "That girl. Where's she off to, I wonder? She's been nothing but trouble since her sister married in June. I don't know what to do with her. She's so rude, and then I say things I don't mean."

"Mothers and daughters, blotters," Elunid intoned.

As nonsensical as the comment was, Bethan had to

agree. God knows they'd had their share of acrimony with their own mother. "Have I offended Isadora in some way?"

"No, no. I fear we have spoiled her since her bout with smallpox. She was so close to death, and we let her behave as she pleased for too long. It's my fault."

"Mrs. Wilson, don't be too harsh with yourself. I would have been lucky to have such a mother as you."

"You're very kind, dear." Mrs. Wilson wiped the corners of her eyes with her apron.

"May I buy some cinnamon buns to take to Lena?"

"Of course. I'll slip an extra one in for your sister."

Elunid gazed out of the window, her lips moving soundlessly.

"Oh dear! I have some puddings in the oven, and no one here to help me get them out."

"I can give you a hand. Elunid, stay put."

When they returned from the kitchen, Elunid had disappeared.

"I'm sorry, lass."

"It's so like her to take off. I'm sure she's not far."

It only took a second for her twin to slip away. She swallowed her rising panic. A few months ago, Elunid had disappeared for an entire day, and had it not been for Henry and George, she didn't know what would have happened.

Henry had carried Elunid home, and at the memory of those strong arms holding her sister with such care, she could not help but imagine what it would feel like to feel protected. Foolish. She did not need protection. She was the strong one.

She scanned Market Street, asking passersby if they'd seen her. Someone pointed toward the docks, where a crowd had gathered, and in the midst of it she saw Elunid with someone wearing a familiar looking slouch hat. Was Freddy still about town? Isadora stood at his side. Oh.

Elunid stood nose to nose with the boy and poked him in the chest. "Because of you, devil, there will be no sunrise tomorrow." She grabbed his jaw and turned it toward the setting sun. "See? You've caused its death with your evil."

Bethan hastened her pace.

"Now, see here, lovey." He laid his hands upon Elunid's upper arms, slid them slowly downward and up again, fingers splayed to graze the sides of her breasts. "I know what you need to calm you down."

Bethan broke through the crowd, and her vision clouding over, slammed her fist into his face. Unprepared for the assault, he lost his balance and fell, head hitting the dock. The crowd scattered out of the way, laughing.

Isadora screamed and ran over to him. "How could you? He meant no harm."

The crowd snickered.

Bethan turned on them. "You saw he was up to no good. Could you not have intervened?"

They backed away. She struggled to slow her breathing.

The chandler said, "It's afraid of her, we are."

"Nonsense. She's never hurt anyone."

Two of the men loomed over Freddy as he got to his feet. "Best ye go, lad."

Bethan put her arm around Elunid's shaking shoulders and wiped the spittle from her mouth with her handkerchief. "Come, sweeting. Let's go home."

As Freddy passed by, the vitriol in his eyes made her draw a breath.

Chapter Five

Bethan hurried Elunid home. She'd begun to tremble, never a good sign.

Lena rushed toward them. "*Mein Gott*! What happened?"

As she sat her sister down by the fire and wrapped a shawl around her, Bethan quickly explained.

"I'll get something to warm her."

Lena soon returned with the soup, and Bethan tried to spoon the broth into Elunid's mouth, to no avail.

Bethan took the packet of medicine Ian had given her from her pocket. "Have you any chocolate?"

Lena nodded and headed for the kitchen.

Elunid rarely refused a cup of chocolate. "Ellie, Ian's herbs might help you in your work. Lena made you a cup. Will you not have some?"

She had mixed the herbs into a quarter cup of chocolate. She covered Elunid's hands around the cup with her own, and Elunid took a sip. The warm drink soon put some color on her face.

As soon as she was finished, Bethan led her into her room. "Let's get you into bed." Mayhap Ian's concoction would be the key to calming Elunid's troubled mind. There was so little she could do for her, but at least she could tend to her physical needs.

"You've gotten so thin, *Chwaer*."

Elunid stood stock still as she put her night rail on.

She tucked her into bed and breathed a sigh of relief. At least she'd stopped shivering.

Lena arrived with a pot of chocolate and two cups. "I knew you'd want to sit with her for a while."

Bethan smoothed Elunid's hair away from her face and tucked the covers neatly at her chest. "Thank you, Lena. Here, my sweeting. It's delicious."

She sat back with her own chocolate, keeping one eye on the cup in her sister's hand, and searched for a passage from Shakespeare. The words filled her mind with calm:

> *"Doubt thou the stars are fire;*
> *Doubt that the sun doth move;*
> *Doubt truth to be a liar;*
> *But never doubt I love."*

Not even the beautiful words from *Hamlet* erased her unease of the consequences of Elunid's encounter with Freddy. If only she could see into her sister's mind as they used to do with each other, then perhaps she would know how to fight her affliction.

Caring for Elunid was like watching a carriage without a driver, helpless to stop its wayward course. She would only tend to her physical needs as best she could.

She snatched the cup slipping from Elunid's hand. "What can I do for you, *Chwaer*?"

"Brush my hair, Mother. Sing your songs."

No use in reminding Elunid Mother had only combed their hair a handful of times, after they came in from the beach with salt water, wind, and adventure in their hair. She'd stiffen and sigh with defeat when they wriggled. Older sister Polly had been the one to mother them and sing to them, too. Mother didn't believe in singing to children.

"It's Bethan."

She settled herself on the bed behind her, took out the pins from Elunid's heavy hair, and let the silken strands fall down her back. She reached for the silver brush on the bedside stand. They had stolen it from Mother's room; perhaps the absence of it made her think of them from time to time.

The steady rhythm of her brushing was like the caress of calm waters on sand. She let her breathing match the rhythm.

"Sing, *Chwaer*."

She hardly recognized the voice rising from her throat; so long had it been since she'd sung. As the songs of their childhood echoed in the room, the tension in her sister's shoulders began to ease, and hers as well, as she recalled their youth, when they'd spent their days wrapped around each other's mind, sharing each other's heart.

"I wonder how you got those tangles. Have you been spinning upside down on your head?"

"Mayhap I should. Might help."

"There. Let me braid it. Are you tired?"

She grunted her assent. "Um."

She rested her palms on the top of her twin's head in blessing, enjoyed the peace in the moment.

"I'll tuck you in now."

When Polly had left them to get married, they'd tucked each other in, until Elunid began to slip away. At least she'd had a moment of peace with her. She would tuck it away in her mind, to smooth away the wrinkles of future pain.

She patted the linen and kissed her on the forehead.

She would fortify herself with a cup of tea and enjoy a moment of solitude before the busy night began.

Chapter Six

If it gave her twin pleasure to see her safely abed, so be it, for there was little else Elunid could give her. The lamentations began after Bethan left, resonating from her belly like a trumpet announcing the coming of war. She'd been idle today, seeking comfort in her sister.

They reveled in reminding her every day she wasted added another day of torment to the souls she sent to hell. She could redeem them if she but created the perfect needlework, the Beauty Stitch. But she had failed them again and again, and another demon joined the chorus, bidding she sink inside herself.

The first tormentor had come in her thirteenth year with the onset of her first courses. Bethan did not suffer from the same gripping pains, the twisting of her womb. The first voice crawled out of her depths then, weaving in and out of her mind like a needle through a cloth, piercing her skin. She could hide the one, even from Bethan. Not now. Not with so many of them, demanding, reprimanding.

The first one, he blew hot and cold, harsh and in turns soft. She couldn't help but listen to him, his seductive voice resonating deep inside her like echoes in a well, never leaving her alone. He was the teacher who schooled her in her guilt, poked her with the needle, whispering praise in one ear when she learned a stitch just so, splattering blood upon the cloth when she failed the Beauty Stitch.

She was so ignorant then, doubted he was truly there. Still she reached out as if blind and traced his cruel lips with her fingers, yearning for his smile. He was the one always within her, while the others might come and go, guiding her in the ways of her penance, making her drift away from Bethan like a boat from the shore.

Chapter Seven

The customers at the inn spoke of nothing else but the tussle at the docks with Bethan and the ne'er-do-well. Henry recognized the little bastard from the description. If only he'd seen it.

The inn was packed with people, the door propped open to let in fresh air. He spotted Bethan bustling around, serving and washing dishes with young Sabine assisting her. George sat at a table by the fireplace with old Captain Jacobs, who tried to teach him the rudiments of chess. He could scarcely believe tomorrow was the boy's eleventh birthday. What a good lad he was: strong, good-natured, kind.

Ed the butcher motioned him over. "I was out there by the docks today, when yon Bethan came barreling down the street and knocked the little bastard off his feet like he was naught but a rag doll."

Old Widow Jenkins cackled. "Not what ye'd call ladylike, but a woman needs to know how to throw a good punch, living in a harbor town."

Ed nodded, clinking mugs with the old woman.

As Henry returned from the kitchen with plates of fried fish, bits of conversation drifted his way.

"Heard the daft one asking the lad who sent him? He laughed and told her no one sent him, but she kept arguing with him."

"Kept calling him lust, or greed, or some such

nonsense. He didn't care for it. Everyone piled up to see what she was going to say next. Ye never know with her."

"It's like a game of chance, it is."

"Young Isadora, what can the chit be thinking, chumming up with the likes of him? If you ask me," Widow Jenkins added, "her father better rein her in, or she'll be in trouble."

"Saw her on the street this evening, father in tow. She had the mark of a hand on her poor ugly face," Ed added.

"Spare the rod and spoil the child," Widow Jenkins said with conviction. "Mayhap she wouldn't be so cranky if they'd taught her to respect her elders."

Henry shook his head. So easy for others to criticize a parent's actions when their children were long grown. You'd think they'd remember what it was like. He set the food in front of the widow with a flourish.

He searched the crowded room again for Bethan. She'd been working steadily since he'd arrived, and probably long before, never stopping to rest, always a smile for everyone. So tall, graceful. Made this old inn bloom with life.

He squinted. As soon as she'd set the platter down, she held her right hand close to her body. Had she tended to it? Probably not. Tended to everyone but herself. She straightened and approached Mrs. Stowe's table.

He joined them and watched Bethan's eyes grow wide at the sight of him. For the love of God, would there be a day she didn't sniff the air when he came near, as if he would walk among civilized people smelling like his labor?

"You've been working hard, Bethan."

She nodded.

He'd gotten a good look at her hand. It was bruised and abraded, and a bit swollen. "Might I have a word with you in private, Mistress Bethan?"

"Must you?" She furrowed her brows.

He folded his arms and gazed at her, then motioned her down the hallway leading to the private rooms.

"Is this necessary?" Bethan scowled.

"Yes, it is. Your hand, the one that collided with the lad's face."

She grinned. "Yes."

He took her arm, felt her stiffen. "You've hurt yourself."

She shrugged, an elegant roll of the shoulders, more like a queen than an ale maiden.

"Bethan, you need ointment and a bandage. It will swell more."

"No time. Let me go, I've things to do." Her mutinous glare would have amused him if she wasn't injured.

He met her gaze. "You need to take it to the apothecary."

"Would you take it for me?" She smirked. "The rest of my body is busy."

"Your entire body?" He couldn't help the path his eyes followed, from her neck to the top of her feet. Amidst the smells of food, sailors, and pipe smoke, her sweet scent filled his senses.

Come now, Henry! "Forgive my impertinence, Mistress Bethan." He would at least allow himself the indulgence of gazing into those darkened eyes. At least she didn't look away.

"I only want you to take a care for yourself. Is your sister well?"

She brightened. "It seems the medicine Ian concocted for her is working. She's abed already."

"Oh, that's grand."

Her smile lit her eyes. His heart thumped and rose from his body, weightless and bright as a hummingbird.

"I'll fetch a bandage and some ointment from Ian."

She pulled her hand away. "Thank you."

****

She lay in bed, willing the lethargy to leave her body. She'd been away from her work too long. The man today where ships go in and out...what was the word? She'd seen the Seven before: Gluttony, Lust, Envy, Greed, Pride, Wrath, and Sloth. Oh, he was Lust. She'd seen them all before, but this time others saw Lust. Was he real? If so, why had he come if not for her?

She could see the completed, perfect work if she closed her eyes: Waves lapping on the bottom of the cloth. The boat holy, blessed by Christ, powerful enough to steer itself. Cedar of Lebanon, shining with sacred light. The sharp tang of saltwater on Peter's face, the apostles, heads ringed with light, the splash of the wave at the bow.

She tried to rise while the vision still burned the back of her eyes. But they had made her arms like the cross, rigid and unyielding, the means for His death. But she couldn't move them, for they had sewn her body down to the cross, stiff as nails, heels stitched to the bed.

How was she to sew the Beauty Stitch when she

could not rise from bed? Because of her, the souls would suffer, the sun would not rise.

Chapter Eight

Lena and Bethan sat at an empty table long after midnight. Lena pushed a plate of fried fish over to Bethan.

"Eat, *Liebchen*. You have earned your keep tonight."

Bethan took off her cap and pulled the pins from her hair, rubbed her aching scalp, one hand bandaged. "Must we clean up tonight?" She eyed the floor with disgust. Tobacco, ale, bits of fish and potatoes were scattered over the wooden planks. "This is the worst mess yet. How have you done this night after night, Lena?"

Lena leaned back and closed her eyes. "It was different when dear Josef was here. Together, it was part of our routine. We gossiped over the news of the night, who'd too much to drink, who we'd caught cavorting. It didn't seem like work."

Bethan chased a bit of fish around on her plate. How wonderful it must have been to have someone with whom to share life's labor, and how bereft Lena must feel without it. She rose and embraced her. "I'm sorry, my friend."

Lena patted her arm. "For Josef's sake and his son's, I must keep the inn going. I like to imagine him—where he is I know not—smiling and yelling at me betimes because I've not done things the way he would." She smiled. "Yet I always knew he loved me, despite his gruff, quiet way."

She sniffed and picked up her ale, wiped the foam from her mouth with the back of her hand. "Um. This might be my best summer ale yet."

Bethan sat again and emptied her mug. "Oh, I agree." She glanced toward the private quarters. "I should go check on my sister."

"You need meat on your bones. Have another mug and eat. The care of your sister wears on you, doesn't it?"

"She's my twin."

"But you must care for yourself."

"Are you and Henry in league?" He whose gentle hands and low voice made her belly quiver.

"Henry? No."

"He said the same thing tonight."

"Ah." Lena brightened, eyes alive with interest. "And…"

"And nothing." She rose. "I must check on Ellie."

She pressed her hand upon the door, and a sense of dread crawled like a spider down her back. She opened the door. In the darkened room, the acrid scent of fear barreled into her.

"Elunid!"

Chanting. A muffled voice chanting, ancient and knowing.

She tripped over something, sent it skittering across the floor. She rushed to light a candle, which illuminated Elunid lying stretched in the bed, arms spread to the sides, fingers splayed, body stiff. The whites of her eyes shone like bone in her ashen face.

"Forgive me. I could not defeat it on my own.

Because I am weak, the darkness is my shame."

"Elunid." Bethan grasped her arm. It was cold as frost. "Pull your arms in, sweeting."

When she didn't respond, Bethan tried with all her might to move them to her sides, but they wouldn't yield. What did this new and frightening development mean?

Panic rose in her throat. "Elunid, we must warm you."

"They've stitched me to the cloth. I cannot move," she rasped. "Two on the shoulders. One on each foot. One on each hand. They will unravel me when I've paid my penance. Be gone, Sister."

Bethan pushed the hair away from her sister's face, fighting a wave of dizzy panic. What must she do? She put the sheets over her as best she could and reached in her pocket for the medicine Ian had given her. He said she could double it.

"I have lost the sun. I'm sorry," Elunid rasped.

"It's okay, *Chwaer.*"

Since Elunid wouldn't move, she could not resist the medicine much. Bethan poured most of her tea out of the cup and mixed the herbs in.

"Those stitches must hurt. This will help."

Before Elunid could resist, she poured the liquid into her mouth. Pray God she wouldn't choke. A bit of it slipped out the side of her mouth, but she swallowed most of it.

Bethan sat on the edge of the bed. "Close your eyes and rest."

Elunid moaned.

She could do nothing but helplessly watch, anger filling her body like black smoke in a chimney. Hours later, as dawn lightened the room, Elunid's limbs began to relax, but her eyelids remained half open.

"The sun has risen, Ellie. All is well."

A spark of awareness lit her eyes, then they drifted shut.

Bethan rose and stretched, her back aching with strain. She took the opportunity to creep into the kitchen for a tray of tea and a bite to eat and returned to sit with Elunid. She must go somewhere to purge the anger roiling inside of her, choking her. Why had God chosen Elunid to suffer so? She murmured the words of the Bard to slow her breathing, but it gave her no comfort.

****

She'd no strength to move, but their whispers rustled like leaves before a storm, rumors of threats and punishments to come. They would return. What was Sister saying? Old words, bold words from the great ugly Bard. Sister lapped up his words like a cat laps cream. How sweet is ignorance when Evil perched in every bit of her body, holding her limbs on the bed.

****

Elunid slept deeply, and if it resembled her other attacks, she would sleep for hours. Had Ian's concoction helped? No, she would not hope, for what was the sense in it? She grabbed her cloak and searched for Lena.

Lena shook her head. "Why did you not wake me, Bethan? I've told you time and again you are not alone in this."

"Don't be angry, Lena."

"You should sleep."

'I cannot. I am going to see Polly. Could you check

on Elunid from time to time?"

"Of course, *Liebchen*. Wait." She handed her a fresh roll from a basket on the table. "If you won't sit down to eat."

She embraced Lena. "Thank you, my friend."

She walked up Siren Street, bleary-eyed from lack of sleep, the muscles in her neck cramping. A walk would do her good. A light breeze from the Channel caressed her back like a tender mother, but how could she enjoy the summer day when her sister suffered so?

Why Elunid? Useless question. God never answered it, no matter how hard she prayed.

The anger enveloped her again, making her cough. Why would a God who was supposed to be merciful let one of His lambs suffer such torment? Why Elunid and not her? God knew she would gladly trade places with her, to spare her the pain. What a little fool she was, to think Ian's remedy could work magic.

She nodded at the butcher hanging his goods but didn't stop to chat, for it would do no one any good to see how angry she was. They would only ask why, and how could she admit she was angry at God?

Once she passed the Landgate, she kept an eye out for ne'er-do-wells camped on the edge of town. How could God create such beauty yet cause such pain and suffering? Elunid had done nothing in her young life to deserve it, and she, her sister, was helpless to prevent it.

Her pace quickened. What was the use of getting angry? She should go see Vicar Andrews. He was a kind man; he could pray for her. No. She couldn't share her innermost, sacrilegious thoughts with him. She would cope on her own as she always did.

The larks sought food from the field, dipped down

and up, twigs in their beaks. The lowing of cattle which normally brought her a feeling of peace only taunted her with elusive normalcy. A bit of blue glimmered through the trees, a calm sea, a perfect day for a picnic, an outing, a fair. Life could be simple for some. Hadn't been simple since Ellie turned thirteen.

When Elunid first started slipping away from her, it was like one of her moods, here one day, gone the next. Over the course of a year, Ellie stopped speaking the secret language they'd had since early childhood. She felt the loss as she would a limb torn from her body. Bethan tried to reach her, but her sister became more and more distant. Then Elunid took up needlework, only speaking of the sins she'd committed and must atone for. With Mother always taking to her bed, it left Bethan and Polly to deal with Elunid's increasingly bizarre behavior.

And she could do nothing for her. She quickened her speed, though her heart beat against her chest like a battering ram. But if she kept moving, she would not scream, would not cry.

She glanced up from her dark thoughts to see she'd gone past her sister's lane and had walked into a thick patch of woods. She struggled for breath and dropped to her knees.

She wheezed, tried to draw air into her lungs through the burning in her chest. *Breathe, Bethan. In and out.* A child's laughter broke through the deafening beat of her heart. There must be a cottage nearby. If she could get to it, breathe through the burn in her chest. If she could get to the cottage, she could rest.

She rose, forced her feet to plod forward. *Don't panic, Bethan. You've not died yet from these attacks.*

But she could, just now.

The child laughed again, accompanied by an answering laugh, deep and rich. She stumbled through the forest toward the sound, came to an edge of a clearing. A small cottage stood, with a wagon a fair distance on the far side. She recognized the wagon. She stumbled to the back of the cottage in the direction of the sound, blinking to clear her fuzzy vision. Nestled among the trees was a pond, steam rising from its waters.

She gasped. Henry, the night soil man, sat upon the bank. He was grinning, hair streaming wet to his shoulders, powerful bare chest covered with black hair. Oh sweet God. He looked like Neptune, mighty and benevolent. And naked. The muscles in his legs tensed and relaxed as he splashed young George. His manhood stood stiff against a thicket of black curls. She tried to suck in air, but a wave of dizziness slammed into her.

Through the buzzing in her ears, a voice called to her from far away, low and resonant.

Strong arms cradled her, naked, and so warm. Her head lay against his chest, the hairs upon it tickling her ear. The muscles of his broad chest were hard and solid against her side, and so reassuring, rising and falling against her, encouraging her to suck in breath. But it was as if she sucked through a hollow reed.

"Bethan, you will be well soon. I'll take care of you."

He smelled of soap and earth. She clasped her arms tighter around his solid neck and closed her eyes. She'd not been held like this since childhood. He began to walk, carrying her as if she weighed no more than a kitten. Heat radiated from his chest, and his stomach muscles shifted and tensed as he headed toward the cottage.

She wheezed, then coughed.

"Don't worry, Bethan. I know what to do."

She nodded, her cheek rubbing against his chest, the curls there soft, yet pleasantly rough. His heart beat a reassuring rhythm against the uneven frantic beat of her heart.

"Georgie has the same problem. I've some herbs will help you. George!" he yelled. "Is there water left in the pot?"

"Aye, Da. What's wrong with Mistress Bethan?"

"She's having trouble breathing, much like you do."

"Da always makes me feel better, Mistress Bethan."

Protected. Safe.

George ran ahead and opened the cottage door. He had a towel wrapped around his waist. He stopped and gaped at them. "Da."

"Not now son. We must help Bethan."

"But Da, you..."

Henry stepped sideways to accommodate Bethan's long legs through the narrow doorway, and she lifted her head, eyes slowly adapting to the dimness in the simple room. A fire glowed in the hearth; a homespun rug lay in front of the fire, with a divan on one side. A simple trestle table stood by the open window. A collection of sea shells and a daguerreotype of a woman graced the mantel.

He stood over the divan. "Can you sit up?" His breath upon her face was warm, his eyes dark.

"Yes." The small effort made her cough.

"You're going to be fine." He leaned over her to put a pillow behind her back, and she gasped. His member nearly rested in her lap. But there was nothing restful about it; it stood stiff and huge against a forest of dark hair. Her nostrils filled with an exotic and earthy smell, as if she'd travelled to a foreign land. And so warm.

He pulled back. "Don't worry. We'll soon set you to rights."

She explored the flecks of hazel in his brown depths.

"Da!"

Henry turned his head. "George, I said not now."

"But…"

With a gentleness that almost made her weep, he put a blanket over her, tucked it under her chin, smoothing the wrinkles. Her body awakened to his light touch.

"Da, you're naked."

"George, be still."

"Naked!"

"What? Oh, dear God."

He backed away, and she saw all of him then: muscular chest, black hair curling around his nipples, and the tight, banded muscles of his stomach, a line of darkness leading to his manhood. But it wasn't resting. It moved. She closed her eyes. She shouldn't be seeing it, but she must. Her eyelids popped open again.

She couldn't remove her gaze from him. She didn't need to breathe, as long as she could look upon him. His eyes followed the path of her gaze.

"Da!" George tapped him on the shoulder, and she came to her senses.

The boy handed him a towel, which he quickly put around his waist. He stood so very close to her, his upper body still bare. "I apologize, Mistress Bethan."

No, he did not look sorry, his lips lifting and a look of man pride darkening his eyes. Why shouldn't he be proud? He wore his body well.

She shouldn't be here. A blush of heat crawled all the way down to her breasts, lingered there at the memory of his hard chest against them. She should be ashamed. What was wrong with her? But without his warm body against her, she felt bereft. Her body grieved the loss of his warm arms around her, his hand gripping the length of her thigh.

"I thought nothing of my nakedness when I saw you crumpled to the ground."

She closed her eyes to avoid his gaze, but her lids opened of their own accord. She watched as he turned around and bent to find something in the cupboard.

He had a broad back and powerful haunches, and the outline of his buttocks behind the towel spoke of hard labor and strength. No wonder he could lift her as if she weighed no more than dandelion fluff.

He returned with a packet of herbs. "George, fill the basin with hot water. Take care not to burn yourself."

George nodded, eyes still wide upon his father.

"Indian tobacco," Henry murmured. "I shan't get dressed until your breathing is better."

She would have laughed had she the breath. *Mayhap I shall not get better if it means I can gaze my fill at you.*

He handed her a linen cloth and bent to put it around her shoulders. "Place this over your head, and

58

breathe the steam. It will help."

She obeyed. She coughed, panic seizing her again.

"Slowly, in and out. There you go."

The low rumble of his voice helped to calm her, as if he still held her to his chest. She breathed in the medicinal vapors, felt her passages slowly open up, and after a while, she was able to breathe deeply. She must remember not to take the simple act of breathing for granted!

George sat at the table, eating out of a bowl. Her stomach rumbled. She'd not eaten anything but the roll this morning.

"Now then." Henry chuckled.

How embarrassing, though why she would worry about such a thing when she'd seen him completely naked...

"George, fetch Mistress Bethan some stew," he said, his gaze still meeting hers. "It's one of my specialties, you see."

"It's the only thing he can make."

Henry winked at her, and she suddenly felt as if she'd plunged from the sky into a bed of feathers.

"Da, you've no shirt on."

He started. "Oh, yes. Again I'm sorry, Mistress Bethan."

"Ye don't sound sorry, Da."

Henry grinned.

She closed her eyes to hide his body from her view, but why bother? His image would forever be imprinted on her mind. She should memorize every detail of it, for she would never have the pleasure of touching him again, the pleasure between a man and a woman her sister Polly hinted at. Her life was dedicated to her twin.

What was she doing here, virtually alone, with a man who made her want more out of life?

She couldn't help watching as he walked away.

"I'll get dressed now if you'll hide your eyes."

Oh, he'd caught her looking. She blushed and turned her head away.

"Better?" He'd put on a pair of simple homespun breeches and held one hand on his narrow hip. His shirt was white against the brown of his shoulders.

"Thank you."

He led her to the table, handed her a steaming bowl of stew, eyes intent upon her. "I hope you like it."

The rich flavor of the broth, tender meat, and the carrots and potatoes did much to revive her. "It's delicious."

He grinned. "If I do say so myself."

"I grew the carrots," George crowed.

"Well done."

She surveyed the small cottage while she ate. It was humble and Spartan, but neat and tidy. Soft morning light bathed the room, and a bookcase in the corner groaned with books.

Henry joined her, and she watched his fingers hold the spoon, his mouth as he chewed.

He stopped. "What's the matter? Have I something on my face?"

"No, no." She must have been staring at him like a dolt.

He grinned. "I see you've finished. Would you like some more?"

She hesitated. "Mother always said my appetite was very unladylike."

"I love to see a woman with a good appetite." His

eyes swept over her face. "Especially when it involves my food."

He filled her bowl and watched as she ate until the bowl was empty.

She was filled with a glorious feeling of well-being. She may as well admit it; it wasn't just the stew.

"Tell me, Bethan, where were you headed before you became incapacitated?"

They had moved back over to the divan, and she laid her head back against the cushion. "I was on my way to speak with my sister Polly."

"Can I help?"

She wanted to taste his face, sink into those warm eyes of his, rich and warm as hot chocolate. She shook her head. "I don't think anyone can."

"Surely it can't be as bad as that."

"I'm afraid it is."

Chapter Nine

Henry resisted the urge to reach over and smooth the crease of worry between her brows. "I'm a good listener."

She glanced at the door. "I should be getting back to Elunid."

"You must rest." She was pale, with beads of sweat on her forehead. "George and I will take you back in the wagon soon enough."

Did she sense his attraction for her? He couldn't let it show; she didn't feel well. Yet, he wasn't so out of practice with a woman's ways that he didn't see her eye his naked body.

"George, would you please make us a cup of tea? You remember how to do it properly, don't you?"

"Surely, Da."

Good lad. He watched with pride as George poured hot water into a teapot, setting it on the hearth, and dropping the tea leaves into it.

Bethan's dark blue eyes widened at the sight of the fine teapot. It was cylindrical, made of red stoneware, with a white flower design and lines etched throughout. It had belonged to Celia, George's mother.

"What an unusual teapot," she murmured.

"It was always one of my favorites," he said.

"From when?"

"Another lifetime ago. As well as being beautiful,

it keeps the tea nice and hot, the way I like it."

George carefully extracted a teacup out of a worn, wood cabinet in the corner. It was light yellow with a pearl luster, and blue flowers. George bit his upper lip with concentration as he carried it over, and with a sigh of relief, set the tea cup and saucer on the table.

"I know what you're thinking."

Her eyes widened. "What do you mean?"

"What's a night soil man doing with such a fine tea service? I've known you long enough to know how curious you are, Mistress Bethan."

She grinned, displaying a charming dimple on her chin. "My mother has always said it would get me into trouble one day." She shrugged. "I can't help it."

"It's a good thing to be curious, for it means we're always learning. It makes life richer, no matter how humble we are." He spread his hands out to take in the room. "You want to know why I would have such a fine set of teaware. Let's just say it was from another place and time."

Her lips twitched. "You are purposely intriguing me."

He smiled. What a fine idea, for it made her focus on him. Seeing the light in her eyes again made a lump rise in his throat.

She bit her lip.

"What is it?"

"You're the most mysterious night soil man I've ever met."

He laughed aloud, making George clatter the teapot.

"I am fairly certain I'm the *only* night soil man you've ever met."

The rich, husky sound of her laughter made his manhood tighten.

"My occupation is only a small part of me."

"I've no doubt, but still…" She pointed toward the bookcase. "For example, so many books. How do you come to be so learned?"

"How do you?" he countered.

She fingered the hem of her apron. "When I was a young child, my mother used to read us stories. We had a fair number of books, because mother came from a fine family. She'd learned to read and taught us. I read every book in the lighthouse. Father used to indulge me by bringing books from his trips."

"You were raised in a lighthouse? How extraordinary."

"It sounds exciting, doesn't it? I love the sea, but the winters are long and brutal, and it was just Mother, Elunid, and myself most of the time. Then father was lost at sea…"

She brightened. "Since Elunid and I have come to King's Harbour, it's been such a joy to have people to talk to, something new happening every day. Who knows what the tide will bring in? At the lighthouse, after Father died, Mother was afraid to let us out. I could only watch the ships go by."

George handed each of them a cup of tea, then plopped down in a chair.

"Thank you, George. What a fine job you've done," Bethan said.

He blushed and smiled.

A comfortable silence fell upon the room as the three sipped their tea.

George slurped the last swallow of his tea. "Da,

may I go outside to check on the nest of baby robins?"

"Yes, but don't disturb them. If you get your scent on them, the mother will abandon them."

George made a valiant attempt at closing the door quietly, but failed.

When Henry turned back to Bethan, his gut wrenched at the despair on her face.

"*Poor robin, gentle robin,*
Tell me how thy leman doth
And thou shalt know of mine."

She sang the old William Cornysh tune in an effortless high soprano. The song echoed in the room long after she finished, desolate and bittersweet.

He touched her hand. "What has made you so sad, Bethan?"

"I was just thinking; sometimes human mothers aren't too different from birds."

"What do you mean?"

She pulled her hand away. "I should be getting back."

"Will you not rest awhile longer, and tell me what troubles you?" He would gladly take the pain from her and carry it himself.

She closed her eyes for a moment, then straightened her shoulders. "My sister has been ill a long time, since the age of thirteen or so. She…sees visions, horrible visions. One day she'll converse with me, be the sister I've always known, and the next she'll be unreachable, in her own hell." She paused and sipped her tea. "I never know what to expect from one day to the next."

He nodded.

"Doctors can do nothing for her. They practically

bled her dry, and the treatments they attempted were cruel and useless." She shuddered. "I cannot help her. I can only watch and wait until it's over. And I fear one day she will sink into madness and never return to me."

He longed to hold her within the shelter of his arms. "How is it you have come to bear the full weight for your sister's care?"

She laughed without humor. "Mother cannot abide by Elunid's 'moods,' as she calls them. She believes Elunid has a choice in how she behaves. She has no power over it, I tell you." She grasped his hands again, nails biting into his skin. No matter, if it gave her comfort.

She cleared her voice and loosened her grip. "I'm sorry."

"No. I'd be angry too, *have* been angry. When George's mother died, I railed against the unfairness of it. And when my family…"

"What?" She leaned forward, dark eyes searching his face.

Should he tell her? To what end? No, this moment was about her pain, not his. "It's a story for another time. Please tell me what happened since I left the inn last night."

Her telling came in waves, anguish growing as the story unfolded. What could he do to ease her suffering?

"I'm sorry, Bethan. It must have been horrible."

She nodded. "And I can do nothing to help her."

"No. But she can depend on you to be there, even when she's not aware."

She drew a shaky breath. "For all it's worth."

"To have the comfort and pleasure of your presence is worth a thousand treasures."

She set her cup in its saucer and brushed nonexistent crumbs off her lap. He had the sudden intense urge to lay his head upon it.

"I've lingered here too long."

Chapter Ten

Here she was, sitting with a man in his home, with only a young boy as chaperone. But what did it matter? The town already considered her unladylike after her encounter with the ne'er-do-well, Freddy. What of it? She would defend her sister above all things. Who cared if they did not approve of her unladylike behavior?

Suddenly, she became aware of a lifting of her spirit, a return to her natural buoyancy. How much of it was due to the comfort of being with Henry, who shared her burden? For the first time in a long time, she felt safe, protected.

"How is your hand feeling?"

She blushed. "You must think me a savage to have hit a man."

"No, Bethan. I think you are both fierce and tender. You do what you must." He seemed to understand the heart of her. How could this be?

"I am often angry. It's not ladylike to be angry."

"You have every reason to be."

"No." She lowered her head.

"What is it?" He lifted her chin.

"I cannot say."

"Whatever you have to say will not shock me. I've been through the fire, Bethan."

The way he said her name, like a caress. "You will

think me the worst kind of person."

"No, I promise you I will not, and I will honor your confidence with my life."

She nodded. Who else could she talk to? "I am angry at God."

No sign of shock, not even a change of expression. He nodded. "Because of your sister."

"Why would he make His beloved daughter suffer so? What did she ever do to deserve such pain? How is it I am well, whole? He's not a fair God." She put her hand over her mouth. "I'll be struck down."

This time, when he put his hand upon her arm in comfort, she let him. "No. For I believe God gave us intelligence, to ponder things, to question our plight and His part in it."

He nodded in the direction of George, who struggled valiantly with the bit as the horse took advantage of his youth and tossed her head around.

"I often had discussions with God, after my first wife died, and as George grew older, and it became obvious he was not normal, and my family... I wondered why He would kill an innocent woman. I tell you, I was angry. You may have heard my second wife died of smallpox. We had only been married six months. One night, when George was six, he touched my face and gazed at me. 'You are sad, Da.'"

"I am, Georgie," I said. "I'm sad God chose to take Jane away from us, that He lets bad things happen."

"Da, don't you see Him?"

"See who?"

"See God. Feel God. He cries with us. He feels sad when we do."

"And as I sat there, I felt the comfort of His

presence. I think what George was saying is God doesn't cause bad things to happen, but He suffers when we suffer. He is with us." He searched her face. "Do you understand what I'm saying?"

She nodded. "It's a lot to think about. I'm glad you're not angry anymore. Young George is an old soul."

"Always has been. I'm thankful for what I have. A healthy, happy son, a worthy occupation, though you may disagree." He grinned. "And a new friend, may I presume?"

"Yes."

His eyes lit up, making her want to bathe in the warmth of them.

"And I promise I won't tell anyone about our conversation." He paused. "Or that you saw me naked."

Chapter Eleven

She ripped her arm away from him.

He shouldn't have said it, but he was only human.

She straightened herself up to her full height, which was impressive, and glared down at him. "You want me to applaud you for doing the right thing?" She turned and stalked toward the wagon, where George sat in the driver's seat.

Did she not know how many men would be happy to spread the news they'd paraded nude in front of a maiden?

She climbed in the wagon, covered her mouth with a handkerchief, stared straight ahead, forbidding as any dowager he'd ever met. Mayhap she wouldn't be as formidable if she knew…no, she must like him and respect him for who he was now. Not who he'd been.

He took George's place at the reins. Once they moved down the lane, the breeze blew any remaining stench from the wagon. She removed the handkerchief from her mouth, her lips pursed with disapproval, but as they rumbled down the lane, the mild summer weather and birdsong made her eyes shine with delight. She wouldn't speak to him again for the remainder of the trip.

No matter, for it was enough to glance over at her and soak in the waters of her dark blue eyes, deep as any lake. And the smooth forehead below her widow's peak, the proud straight back and the strength of her.

"Bethan, would you like to stop at your sister Polly's?"

She frowned. "No, I must get back to Elunid. Besides, I don't care to explain to her how I ended up at your cottage…"

"Da," George called from the back of the wagon. "Why don't I have a granny?"

This was new. "Why do you ask, lad?"

"Robbie's granny lets him eat bread and jam, and he gets to spend the night with her. She takes him to the fair sometimes."

"And you would like a grandmother too."

"Yes! Where is mine, Da?"

He hadn't anticipated this question and let a moment or two go by while he struggled for an answer. He would not lie to the boy, exactly. But neither could he tell the whole truth.

"Your grandmother lives far away."

Bethan stared at him. Something in his voice must have given him away.

"Can we visit her? I should like to meet her, Da."

"I'm sure you do, but it's too far to travel at this time."

"All right, Da."

Damn. He couldn't bear to hear the disappointment in the boy's voice. He seldom asked for anything. But he couldn't tell the boy his grandmother didn't want him.

He longed to unburden himself with someone. Would Bethan understand? But then he would have to tell her everything.

"Da."

"Yes, George."

"I just thought of something. I would have two grannies, wouldn't I? The mother of you, and the mother of my mother in heaven."

"Yes."

He'd been so intent upon their conversation, he hadn't heard the racket of the oncoming wagon until it was just behind them.

"Well, they're dangerously close. They've got a lot of nerve," Bethan murmured. "What's their hurry?"

"Fancy carriage," George exclaimed. "Look at the horses! They must be important people."

"Well, then. We must let them pass." Henry pulled the carriage to the side of the road.

As the carriage overtook them, a man with a great plumed hat stuck his head out the window. "Your horse is so ugly, I don't know whether you're going backward or forward."

"Silly louts," Bethan said. "Never think of anyone but themselves."

"I've rarely heard an unkind word fall from your lips, Bethan."

"Experience."

What would she think of *him* if she knew? He let the horses graze alongside the road. "Tell me."

She avoided his gaze. "It's in the past. No sense bringing it up now." She folded her arms.

"Do you dislike all aristocracy?"

"They're useless. Shallow. Selfish." She stared straight ahead, lips pressed together.

George patted her shoulder. "Don't be upset, Mistress Bethan."

She leaned her cheek against his hand. "You're

right, young George. It's too lovely of a day."

Just as they passed the Landgate, the Wayfaring Wastrels sallied out of the Ale House.

"Look who's back, George!" Bethan said.

"Yes," he crowed. "Master Reginald and the China Doll!"

Reggie, the leader of the travelling musicians, held the arm of Charlotte, the petite songstress with the voice of a temptress. Not his type, though. He liked his women tall and statuesque. His woman. If only it could be so.

"Oh ho, Mistress Bethan!" Reggie abruptly broke away from Charlotte and bowed. "The sun has kissed your face in the most alluring manner."

She smiled, pink-cheeked. "You're back. How were your travels?"

Henry didn't care for the delight in her voice, and the smile clearly not meant for him. And she didn't look at the dandy like he'd shite on his face. *Stop, man. You've no claims on her.*

"Reggie, good to have you back in town." His smile felt stiff and must have looked even more so.

The musician made him feel like a humble man indeed, with his fine coat and all the accessories of a young dandy. Truth be told, Reggie cut a masculine figure in the dark blue suit, hair neatly tied back. He approached the wagon.

"Henry, a pleasure indeed. Hallo, Georgie!"

"Hallo, Master Reggie." George hopped out of the wagon and stood in front of him.

He tousled the boy's hair. "Have you been singing?"

"Oh yes."

"The decent songs anyway," Henry said.

Reginald turned toward Bethan. "You are summer itself, in all its ripe beauty." He had the temerity to meet her gaze. Lout.

"Er, and you, Mr. Reginald."

"Oh please, call me Reggie. All my friends do." His eyes were very dark under even darker brows, his cheeks lean and nose straight. The ladies seemed to swoon around him; he radiated an element of danger which seemed to attract them. What about Bethan?

He kissed her hand, and she turned her head away. Then she blushed, a clear radiant pink, like the inside of a sea shell.

Charlotte tugged on his sleeve. "Reggie, let's go to our lodging."

Her bodice was laced tighter than the strings on a smuggler's bundle, and her ample breasts all but tumbled out. A man couldn't help but stare.

Bethan snatched her hand away from Reggie's grasp. Hurrah!

Reggie continued to gawp at her.

"Reggie!"

He rolled his eyes. "Yes, your highness."

Bethan had rallied, and now her eyes were alight with amusement, bringing out specks of green, like fresh summer grass on a lawn.

Reggie brought his hat to his chest and bowed. "Your servant, madame."

George giggled and bowed, a perfect imitation of Reggie. "Your servant, madame."

Bethan laughed. He'd give up a kingdom to make her laugh in such a way.

Reggie and Charlotte walked arm in arm, singing a

merry tune, George following them down the road. Henry urged the horses on.

Bethan sat upright in the wagon, a dreamy expression on her face. Did she have a soft spot for the wastrel? He cleared his throat, and she glanced at him, lifting one eyebrow. Waited.

"I don't presume to tell you what to do, Mistress Bethan, but might I give you a bit of advice?"

She smirked. "Because of your vast experience in the world?"

She thought him the lowliest of species. He would not react.

To her credit, she said, "I'm sorry. It was a mean-spirited thing to say."

"I know it's not your way." He nodded toward Reggie. "Yon Master Chevalier uses women and tosses them away like an empty mussel shell. As Shakespeare says, 'Some report a seamaid spawned him and some, that he was begot between two stockfishes.' "

She burst out laughing. The folks on the street turned to stare.

She looked him full on this time and smiled, making a dimple dance on her left cheek.

He had the odd sensation of being lifted high into the air, then spun like a top. He blinked to get his bearings.

"Angelo, the lout. Reggie seems harmless enough to me." She tilted her head, eyeing him.

Was she teasing him? She could not see how breathtaking she was.

"You need watching over."

She bristled then, smile fading. "I'm quite capable of taking care of myself, and my sister as well."

"He's not an honorable man."

"I'll decide for myself."

"Clear the way, man! Do your courting off the road." A farmer with a load of turnips yelled.

She must think him a real gawk; he'd stopped the wagon again without realizing it. In an awkward silence, they travelled the rest of the way to the Siren Inn.

"My sister, I'm sure she's awake by now and wondering where I am." She scrambled down from the wagon before he had a chance to help her, making him look like a right dolt. She stopped, smoothed her skirt, clasped her hands in front of her. "Thank you for your help today," she said formally.

He nodded. "I'll be in presently to help with the evening's meal. You can't get rid of me quite yet, Mistress Bethan."

He would watch over her whether she liked it or not.

Chapter Twelve

Upon her arrival, Bethan found Elunid sitting with Lena in her private parlor, staring at the fire, needlework in her lap.

"She's fine. Woke up as if nothing ever happened," Lena whispered. "Didn't mention you. I can't get her to eat, though. Little Josef eats more than she does." The babe suckled at her breast, one chubby hand on her white flesh.

Bethan put her hand on her sister's shoulder. "Hello, Elunid."

Elunid lifted one eyebrow. "How is the brown one?"

"What?"

Elunid sniffed delicately. "Yon shite master. You've been with him."

Lena glanced up. "*Vas ist das*?"

Bethan sniffed her clothes. "I do not stink."

Elunid grinned. "I never said you did."

That was her sister: unhinged one minute and lucid the next, just long enough to bedevil her. She would spend a lifetime puzzling over her, no doubt. She poured herself a cup of tea. She might as well enjoy this moment of normalcy.

"Yes, Elunid. I know you have a preternatural sense of smell."

Her twin met her gaze, and Bethan had the oddest

feeling of looking at herself in the mirror. "There's a warmth about you, *Chwaer*."

"No, I'm not warm at all."

"Yon shite master."

"Would you kindly stop calling him that?"

"It matters not what he does. He warms your blood." Elunid fanned the air in front of her face. "I can feel it."

Elunid's current mood recalled their childhood days, when they felt the other's emotions as if they were their own, and finished each other's sentences.

Lena chuckled, dislodging the baby from her nipple. He squawked, and she set him to rights again. "Oh, you carry a torch for Henry? I thought as much."

"I do not!"

"You wait for him every morning to come by. Don't think I don't know why you rise so early. Then you light up like the sunrise."

Elunid stage-whispered, "She thinks she's too good for him, because of what he does. Yet she would be a midwife, dealing in women's muck."

"Well enough, Elunid." In truth, she'd never thought of it that way. No man she knew would get anywhere near the mess and smell of birthing a baby. When she'd helped Maggie deliver her sister Polly's twins, she'd been so busy helping she hadn't noticed the mess, until after. Elunid did have a point. Not that it was any of her business.

"The Wandering Wastrels are back in town."

"*Ach*, silly Charlotte. She's so demanding, you'd think she was royalty." Lena smiled, showing the dimple in one plump cheek. "But Reginald, he makes me laugh. And his voice…"

How good to see Lena smile. If he could bring her friend joy, he must not be as bad as Henry seemed to think. Mayhap he was just jealous. Jealous? But why would he be jealous over her, a gawk of a girl? Mother reminded her how masculine and clumsy she was often enough. But she didn't feel so when he'd held her in his arms. Never mind.

"How long will they be in town? They do liven up the place." Lena put the babe on her shoulder to burp him.

"Seems they may be here for a while."

"Wandering Wastrels," Elunid murmured. "W. Double U. I don't much care for the letter 'W.' Wandering Wastrels. The letter 'W' consternates me. It lacks logic, and if you say it over and over..." Her brows creased in indignation.

"Please don't. I haven't thought about the letter 'W' since I learned it. Other things on my mind."

"Don't I know it. But double U."

Lena shook her head. "*Liebchen.*"

"Good Lord, Sister. Let's change the subject to getting food into you. You're skin and bones."

"I have no appetite."

"Force yourself. I'll get you some more cinnamon buns if you eat the rest of the soup."

"You lie."

"No, sweeting. I promise I'll fetch some for you. Three."

Her eyes lit up and Bethan swallowed the bittersweet lump in her throat, for the memories of what life used to be.

Elunid took a spoonful and scowled.

"You don't like my soup?" Lena eyed her.

"No indeed."

"Elunid!" Bethan poked her.

"It's gone cold, is all."

"Well, whose fault is that?" Lena huffed.

Elunid shrugged. "Mine." She picked up her spoon, finished her soup, and said not another word.

****

Later that evening, Bethan leaned against the counter and regarded the crowded room. Good thing Henry and George were there, for the inn was jam-packed with hungry customers. Lord Toff and his merry band of macaronis had deigned to join the revelry. He had the look of Davyd about him, the white blond hair, the way he surveyed the room like his personal kingdom. Set her teeth on edge. She plunked a tray of ale on the table.

Lord Toff eyed the mug with suspicion. "Is this drinkable?"

"You'll not find better ale anywhere."

"We'll see." He eyed her with speculation, the arrogant bastard.

"Will you be eating, sir?"

"Depends on what's edible." He licked his lips, eliciting laughs all round.

"All the food is good."

"Bring me your best victuals," his companion said.

She turned without comment, and relaxed her clenched fists.

She soon returned from the kitchen in time to see Reginald and Charlotte sing a duet for small coins, a raucous one she'd not heard before.

"Love those Roman fingers,
Love your wicked grin

Love the things you do to me
Be it out or in."

The two bowed amidst catcalls and whooping, and Reggie motioned to Lena. "My lovely, a flagon of mead, if you please."

Lena giggled like a girl. "My pleasure, Reginald."

Interesting.

The inn's door opened, letting in a well-needed rush of cool air. Maggie Pierce waddled into the inn with Ian behind her in his travelling chair. A crowd gathered around them.

"What in hell?" Widow Jenkins hobbled over, one hand behind her bent back.

"This travelling chair is serving me well, though I've shaken my melon from the trip over the cobblestones."

"Mayhap 'twill do you good," Widow Jenkins yelled.

Ian grinned. "Mayhap." He took Maggie's hand, and Bethan caught the warm and private look they gave each other.

She swallowed the envy rising in her throat like bile. No time to dwell on what she'd never have, for with the arrival of the apothecary, the din had gotten even louder, and it seemed he'd brought the thirst out in everyone. Being limited to the wheelchair in no way lessened his vitality. He'd grown massive in the shoulders and chest, and his green eyes glittered with mischief as he searched the crowd.

He kissed Maggie's hand. "Come, my ripe beauty. I'll buy you a mug of summer ale."

"No need to play the swain with me, husband."

"I will always be your humble servant, for you

saved me from the brink of death." He placed his hands upon her ample stomach. "And you are giving me a child."

"Can you not save your sentiment for when we're alone?"

He boomed, "Why should I not shout my love to the world? You are my joy, my savior."

At this point, the room had gone quiet, waiting, as Bethan was, to see what the man would do next. It was almost as much fun watching Maggie's discomfiture as watching Ian.

Widow Jenkins gasped. "Savior! How sacrilegious! You'll go to hell, young man."

"No doubt. And I'll gladly go to hell as long as she's there, warming my bed."

"There's no cavorting in hell, fool! And none in heaven either."

"More's the pity. Are you entirely sure, Mistress Jenkins?"

Maggie looked at the ceiling, snatching her hands away." Give me patience, Lord."

Bethan eyed the midwife's stomach carefully. It seemed to have dropped lower, so when Maggie walked over to a corner table, Ian behind her, she could barely walk.

"I'm sorry, sweeting." Ian managed to pull the chair out for her. "I was so busy bedeviling you, I left you on your feet too long. You look like you're going to topple over."

She gave him the gimlet eye as she plopped down. "*Thank* you."

Bethan happened to catch Reggie's eye. What ailed the man? For he wore a wistful look upon his face as he gazed at Maggie and Ian.

Charlotte stood with her arms folded, no doubt miffed at the crowd's fickle attention span. She stalked past Lord Toff's table.

"Madame, your voice is heaven sent," he announced.

She stopped and preened. "I thank you."

"Have we not seen you in London?"

"It's possible."

"Have you been to the palace?"

"Yes, a time or two."

"What are you doing in this godforsaken little place?"

"I'll ask you the same thing."

Bethan turned away. Shallow. Selfish.

Ed the butcher ran his hands over the arms of Ian's chair. "Who made this contraption?"

"My good friend Henry. Skilled, is he not?" Ian said.

"Like a work of art, it is."

"Yes, and very useful for things like this." Ian leaned over and kissed Maggie's cheek.

She smiled and patted his cheek. "Feed me."

Bethan hurried to the kitchen and grabbed a bowl of oyster stew and a large slice of brown bread.

Maggie thanked her and dug in.

"How did Henry manage to build this?" Ed asked.

"I drew him a picture, but I had no idea he planned to make one. I'd seen a few on the continent in my travels."

Reggie put a hand on Ian's shoulder. "Aye, and now you'll be seeing them everywhere in Britain."

"So, you've returned like a bad ha'penny."

"To torment you, old friend."

Ian and Reggie had sung together and travelled the world for many years together as the Wandering Wastrels.

"Ah, there's the artist himself." Ian clapped his hands.

Henry appeared carrying a giant tray of mussels and oysters and nodded briskly to Ian as he set the tray on a nearby table. Bethan smiled her thanks as she took the plates to be distributed among the crowd.

"Come on, Henry. Take a bow for your artistry."

Bethan held one last plate and leaned against the wall to catch her breath.

Henry wiped the sweat off his forehead. "I don't have time for lollygagging now, Ian. Can't you see there's work to be done?"

He turned to face her, and suddenly he stood before her, water dripping off his naked body, steam rising from his broad chest. He stood so close she could breathe him in—pine, soap, man. Black curls covered him from chest to taut stomach. She wanted to run away—and toward—the wild heat of him, his member standing straight against a thicket of black. Her center burned, surged through her body, rising to the tips of her fingers, willing her to answer the call of his skin.

Hands upon her arm. "*Liebchen,* are you well? You're standing here with your eyes closed."

She'd dropped the plate, all eyes on her, murmurs of concern and amusement buzzing like wasps.

"Are both sisters touched, then?"

Mayhap she *was* losing her mind. No.

"Don't worry, Lena. I'm fine. I just got dizzy for a moment." Yes, dizzy with lust. She couldn't deny it now.

"You need to sit down for a minute. You're overtired, I think." Lena led her toward the private quarters.

"Mistress Bethan, are you ill?"

Henry's gaze upon her face made her pulse race again, his fully clothed body solid and strong as a fortress. Could he guess she'd conjured up his naked body?

"No need to fuss over me," she mumbled.

"I say, mistress. Can I trouble you for another mug of…?"

"One moment," she barked. "Demanding, privileged bastards."

Lena gave her a warning glance. "Bethan!"

Henry pulled her into the kitchen. "What is it? You're distraught. Do you know this man?"

Why should she resist the pleasure of being close to him? She leaned her forehead against his broad shoulder and breathed in the comforting warmth of him, the homey scent of baked bread and ale.

"I knew someone like him, long ago."

"He was not good to you?"

Lena rushed in and filled a pitcher with ale. "You must rest, Bethan. Go out to the courtyard and get some air."

Bethan let Henry lead her outside.

He brushed off the stone bench. "Sit down. Talk to me, Bethan."

Why not tell him? "I grew up with a boy named Davyd. He was one of the local gentry. We played together on the beach, before Mother became too afraid to let us out. We were the merry three."

He listened as if his life depended on it and put his hand over hers.

"Davyd went away to school and returned every summer. He witnessed Elunid's worsening condition, vowed his love for me, told me he would help me save her. I believed him. A few years passed, and my mother gave me an ultimatum. I was to see to Elunid, or she'd send her away."

"You were young to have such a burden on your shoulders."

"He promised. He said he would find a place for her. He said he loved me and would take care of us both, and like a fool I believed him. I so wanted to have someone take care of me."

"You were young."

"And desperate." She shrugged. "When he returned, we made a plan for the three of us to slip away one night. He would marry me, take care of Elunid."

She held tighter to his hand. "We waited on the beach that night, hour after hour. It was cold, and Elunid pointed to her visions in the sea, and the sun rose on my despair. I never heard from him again. Breeding overcame love, as it always does with the aristocracy."

"I'm sorry, Bethan."

She nodded. "My mother arranged to have Elunid sent to a distant relative who was 'not afraid of a young girl's moods.' Elunid changed their tune in no time. A month later, they dropped her at our door. It's when we went to Polly's."

"I see."

"So the sight of an arrogant toff setting himself

above all others rankles me."

"I wish I could take your pain away."

Bethan wiped her eyes, lifted her chin. "So now you know." She walked into the inn without another word.

Chapter Thirteen

By the end of the evening, a few of the faithful still gathered at the inn. Vicar Andrews slid into a seat by the window. Bethan hurried toward him, a mug of summer ale at the ready.

"Ah, good evening, Mistress Bethan." He smiled.

She resisted the urge to adjust his wig just a tad. "You're looking very cheerful this evening."

"Ah. I finished Sunday's sermon, and may I just say I was inspired?" His hazel eyes searched her face. "Will you be attending?"

She put her weight on one foot. "I'll try."

He nodded and glanced about the room. "Is Mistress Sabine well? Ah, there she is." Two spots of color appeared on his cheeks as he clearly watched Sabine, Lena's adopted daughter, lean against the corner table, her one-year-old daughter on her slender hip. Sabine came from the Orient, and had been taken in by Lena and Josef the year before.

Everyone in town knew Vicar pined after Sabine. She took pity on him and joined her, feeling like a giantess next to her petite form. She reached for the baby.

Sabine smiled shyly. "Thank you."

"I've been tallying up how much Maggie's eaten." Bethan tipped her head in the midwife's direction. "Three bowls of oyster stew, three plates of mussels, an entire loaf of bread, and some haddock."

Sabine giggled, and despite her fatigue, Bethan couldn't help but join in.

"Would you mind getting Vicar Andrew's order?"

Sabine grew very still upon seeing him. He smiled, set his mug down too hard, and splashed ale on his face.

She giggled again and nodded. "Vicar," she enunciated.

"Yes, well done!" Bethan smiled. Sometimes life could be as simple as two people drawn to each other.

Emma Spark's brother burst through the door.

"She's having the babe, Mistress Maggie! They sent me to fetch you. I didn't know my sister knew all those curse words."

"Like what, Ethan?" Ian beckoned him over.

He leaned down and whispered into Ian's ear. "She said, and…"

Ian roared with laughter. "Creative."

"That's quite enough." Maggie stood, holding the table for support. "Fine for you to laugh at the pain of a birthing mother. Try having a baby sometime. See if you make sport of it then, pip."

Ethan backed away as she approached him. "Sorry, Mistress Maggie."

She huffed and gave Ian a dirty look. "Let's go, then."

"Woman, you're not delivering a baby tonight. Look at you, you can barely walk."

"I can still do my job."

"I'll fetch your sister."

She leaned toward Ian. "You know my sister is not…able."

He nodded.

Bethan rushed forward. "I'll go with you." She glanced at Lena. "Is it okay?"

"We'll finish up, George and I." Henry settled Bethan's cloak around her shoulders. "There's a wind blowing in from the Channel."

Ian wheeled the chair around.

"Stay here, husband. It's late for you to be using your chair in the streets."

He scowled. "I'll not have you walking about town without me at this hour. And if you think I can't protect you just because I'm in a wheelchair, you are mistaken, my love."

She sighed. "Come on, then."

"Tell the lass we'll pray for her delivery," Widow Jenkins called. "E'en though the honeymoon came before the wedding." She cackled, amidst a round of laughter.

"And that's never happened before in this town," Maggie said.

The cool air carried the scent of the sea and the promise of a late summer storm. At least it doused the warmth of her shoulders where Henry had touched her when he'd put on her cloak.

They gingerly made their way over the cobbles. Ian picked up the rear.

"Maggie, there's no need to rush."

"Well, there may be."

"It's not worth you exhausting yourself. You've the babe to think of."

"Dare I say he's right?" Bethan added.

"There's no way of telling how long a first birth may take. More than likely it will take hours, but there are exceptions." She stopped. "Have you the endurance for it, Bethan?"

"Without a doubt, Mistress Maggie." She had the endurance to withstand her sister's affliction, why not for her birthing women?

"I'm a bit concerned about young Emma." Maggie stopped to catch her breath. "She's only fifteen and has been the spoiled darling of both her mother and father. Her hips are narrow, and we can only pray the child's not overly large."

Bethan nodded. "I will help however I can."

When they reached Emma's cottage, her young husband answered the door. "Come in. She's cursing at me, and I can't get her to stop."

"Yes, Tom." Maggie put a reassuring hand on his shoulder. "It's what delivering mothers do. Don't worry, it won't last."

His chubby face brightened. "Come in. Her mum's got the room ready for ye." He stared at Maggie's belly, eyes round as a full moon. "Mistress, are you able…"

"Of course I am," she snapped.

He looked behind her. "Oh hallo," he said to Bethan.

"This is my assistant, Bethan."

"I don't know anything about this business but won't she have to bend over a long way, to catch the baby?" He addressed Bethan, then glanced at Maggie apologetically. "It's just…you'll have to stand so far away, how can you reach?"

Maggie's eyebrows rose. "No wonder your wife calls you names." Without another word, she walked regally over the threshold.

Bethan made a valiant effort to keep from grinning, but failed.

Her nervous hilarity was quelled at the sight of Emma sitting up in bed, brown eyes huge in a pale face. And who wouldn't be frightened? Even a young girl like this one knew women died during their travails.

Tom approached the bed and stroked Emma's hair.

Mistress Evans, Emma's mother slapped his hand away. "Be gone with you, lout! Could you not have waited a few months, you and your lust? Now look what you've done to her." She held her daughter's hand again. "Poor baby."

"Ease off, Mum. There were two of us doing it. And I liked it, I did."

"I wasn't going to say it." Ignoring her mother's venomous stare, Tom bent to kiss her flushed forehead. "Dear Emma. I love ye, I do."

She nodded, and a pain came upon her. Just as quickly, she scowled at him.

Ian stuck his head in the door, much to the shock of the mother. "Maggie love, I'm going to fetch your basket and the model." He smiled at the boy. "Don't worry, lad. Steady as she goes."

"Take a care for yourself, husband."

He nodded. "Freddy, walk with me to fetch what your wife needs. We'll bring my lute as well. Bid your love adieu."

He smoothed the damp hair from her face. "Emma, I'll return soon."

She paid him no heed as he shut the door behind him.

"Let's see how we're getting along, shall we, Emma?"

Emma clutched the blankets, knuckles white as parchment.

"Who's this'un?" Emma's mom pointed to Bethan.

"I'm Bethan Owens, mistress."

"Ah, you're Polly's sister."

"Yes, ma'am."

She glanced at Maggie. "Not the touched one, I hope."

"Of course not," Maggie snapped.

"Aren't ye a bit young to be doing this?"

"She may be young, but she's already showing great promise, and as my sister's overly busy with that daughter of hers, I'll soon be needing a substitute."

As if in answer, the babe within Maggie rolled over and created such a hubbub, they couldn't help but stare. Did it have a playmate in there?

Maggie patted it. "Now then." She turned to her mother. "Have you any almond oil?"

Her mother nodded and reached in the dresser by the bed. She handed it to Maggie.

Bethan took in every gesture, every word Maggie said, her tone of voice and confident, deliberate movements.

"Now then, Emma. I'm going to examine you to see how far your birthing passage is open. Breathe deeply. Don't worry. I won't take long."

Maggie poured almond oil on one hand and lifted the girl's night rail.

She grunted as she tried to lean over the bed. "There must be some way…ack!" She reached her arms toward Emma but could not reach her due to her bulging stomach. She cocked her head and eyed the bed. She turned sideways and leaned forward, face red with exertion. "Even if I have her get on the floor, I could not manage to reach her." She turned to Bethan, eyebrows beetled with defeat.

Bethan couldn't help it. She rushed to put her hand over her mouth to prevent the giggle bubbling up, but failed.

"Mistress *Bethan*, what is it you find so amusing?"

The baited bear Bethan had seen at the county fair seemed like a lamb compared to Maggie's fierce demeanor.

"I'm sorry, Mistress Maggie."

Just then, another labor pain saved Bethan from Maggie's wrath. She rushed to Emma's side. "Take my hand. Squeeze it. Breathe."

Emma twisted in the bed, as if she could escape her ordeal.

Bethan's advice came from deep inside. "Don't fight it. Breathe, Emma. Your body is opening up for your child."

"It's killing me."

"No, you'll be fine. This pain will be over soon. Just get through this pain, that's all."

Emma nodded, looking Bethan in the eye, screaming as the pain crested.

"Well done, Emma." Bethan laid a cloth on her forehead and glanced at Maggie.

"Well, I hadn't planned on this, but obviously I'm more immense than I thought. Bethan, you must check Emma and fast before another pain comes. I will instruct you."

Maggie handed her the almond oil and led her to the foot of the bed.

Bethan fought her rising panic. She'd anticipated helping Maggie, but now she would actually be delivering the child. Her heart beat in her throat, and she breathed deeply to put it back where it belonged.

"Apply the oil liberally on one hand. Insert two fingers. Do it quickly and don't hesitate."

Emma cried out.

"I'm sorry," Bethan cried.

"Don't apologize," Maggie whispered. "It will just make her more fearful."

Whatever squeamishness she might have had when thinking about such an activity vanished with Maggie's steady, calm voice.

"Don't hesitate. That's right."

"Normally the inner passage is tight and narrow. You should feel a thinning and a widening of the passage. How far apart can you hold your fingers? Remember the distance. Now, remove your hands."

When Bethan turned to Maggie, she held her thumb and forefinger three inches apart.

Maggie nodded. "Emma, you're progressing nicely. You're doing very well. Your mother will give you a poached egg in broth to strengthen you."

Bethan covered her up again and wiped her hands upon her apron.

"I'm scared," Emma moaned.

"I know. We all must endure this, and so will you," Maggie said.

"If you'd kept your skirts down for your worthless husband, you'd not be suffering now," her mother hissed.

A pain slammed into Emma, and Maggie shot the mother a censorious look. "You will only speak when you've something nice to say."

"Such high hopes we had for you, with your beauty, and you opened your legs for the first man who looked at you.'

"I love him, Mum."

"You'll soon see how sorry you'll be."

Maggie took Mistress Evans' arm. "Enough. You're here to give her comfort, not to abuse her. Keep your mouth shut, or you will step out. Do you understand?"

Emma's mother lowered her eyes, and Bethan marveled at the absolute authority Maggie had over the situation. Could she ever do the same?

Chapter Fourteen

"Fetch the broth and egg now, Mother." Maggie ordered.

"Aye."

When she'd left the room, Maggie stood beside Bethan. "It's not easy for a mother to see her daughter suffer. Oftentimes, they just need something to occupy their hands."

Emma lay with her eyes closed. Bethan strode to the window where a cradle stood. "What a lovely cradle, Emma."

"My Tom made it."

"He's a skilled carpenter. And I see you have a lovely blanket ready."

"I sewed it myself."

"Between the two of you, the babe will be well cared for."

A grimace soon marred the glowing pride on Emma's face as another pain came upon her.

Bethan approached the bed and grasped the girl's hand. "Deep breaths, Emma. It will soon be over."

"You lie, mistress!" She gasped.

"Your passage is stretching for your wee one with each pain, girl." Maggie's soothing voice served to calm Bethan as well.

She too must learn to speak with such assurance. "Try to think only of this pain, how you will breathe through it."

Emma nodded, and Bethan wiped her sweat-drenched face.

"That's right." Maggie stood at the foot of the bed, hand on the small of her back.

"Maggie, why don't you sit?"

'No, I'm fine."

She nodded. Just then, Emma's mother arrived with Maggie's basket and handed it to her. Maggie rummaged through it and held out what appeared to be a cloth ball. Mistress Evans gave Emma a sip of broth and wiped her face with a cool rag.

"Do you remember the model I showed you? It will mean more to you now." Maggie waddled over to the other side of the bed and held up a cloth model somewhat resembling a large walnut. "This is your womb." There was an opening at the bottom. "See the hole in the bottom? That is your privy passage."

She pressed the womb at the top, and the privy passage widened. "When you have a pain, the force of it widens the passage, see? And the pains increase in strength and come closer together. They will become more powerful, and the baby will emerge." She pushed on the womb, and the babe emerged, head first, arms and legs crossed in front of its body.

Understanding lit Emma's face, then another pain assaulted her. When it abated, she gasped. "Will it soon be over?"

Maggie laid her hand on Emma's thin shoulder. "I won't lie to you. The pains will increase in power, but you will find the strength."

"I can't do it." Emma turned her head to the wall.

Mistress Evans took her daughter's face in her

hands. "You will bring this babe into the world, as I did you."

Emma nodded, and she grabbed her mother's hands as another pain bore down on her.

"Squeeze my hands, love. I'd take this pain from you and bear it myself if I could."

After the next pain was over, Maggie told Bethan to check Emma's progress.

With a little more confidence than before, Bethan inserted her fingers. "Oh!"

"What is it?" Maggie asked.

"It's the head. I feel the head." She withdrew her fingers. "Emma, I felt the baby's head!"

"Oh God! He's killing me." Emma moaned as another pain crested.

"Emma, it is almost over now. You will hold your babe soon."

A chill crept up Bethan's neck at the sound of Emma's animal-like groaning, rhythmic and primitive. How to help in the face of such agony?

As if she'd read her mind, Maggie put her hand on Bethan's arm. "It seems impossible, yet it is done every day."

"Are you frightened for your own ordeal, Maggie?"

"I would be daft if I wasn't." Maggie placed her hands on her stomach, took a deep breath. "But we do what we must do. Now then, Emma. It's time to push. Your privy passage is ready, but it's best if you have the urge."

"The urge," she gasped.

"Yes, you will feel as if you…"

"I can't shit *now*!"

"That's it. With the next pain, you must push from deep within your belly, Emma."

"Oh God, I'm splitting in two."

"Here comes another contraction, Bethan. Put a pillow behind her back, Mother."

"Sweeting, squeeze my hand. It will be over soon."

"Emma, when you get the urge, take a breath from deep within your belly, and push," Bethan urged. "Every push brings your baby closer to you."

Emma gritted her teeth.

"Breathe, Emma." Bethan had to raise her voice above the moaning.

You breathe too, Bethan. Don't hold your breath.

Bethan spread some oil around the opening, massaging it as she'd seen Maggie do with her sister, Polly.

Emma grunted, her face red with the effort of pushing. The head emerged and then receded.

Bethan glanced at the midwife.

"This is normal," Maggie said.

The pains had increased in strength and duration, and the room grew silent, but for Emma's moans. How could such a slip of a thing endure the pain for hours on end? She screamed as another pain took hold.

"Almost over, Emma. Hold your breath and push."

This time the head did not recede. "Well done, Emma."

No response, eyes closed. Had she fainted?

"She's so weak," her mother whispered.

"Give her a spoonful of broth," Maggie urged.

But there was no time.

"Push, Emma."

"Squeeze my hands, love."

"I can see the baby's hair, Emma. Push."

Emma pushed, and Bethan felt the force of power as the baby's shoulders emerged partway. The room filled with strength, unearthly and raw.

"Holy Sister," Maggie intoned. "Help this mother and child."

"Oh God," the mother moaned. "My poor baby."

"You are strong, Emma. One last push. A hard push," Maggie urged.

"You must rotate the shoulders so she doesn't tear."

As Emma pushed, Bethan struggled to hold onto the slippery body as it slid out of Emma. Maggie handed her a linen cloth. The baby was dusky blue and not breathing.

"Here, rub him with the cloth, like this." As Maggie did so, the babe gave out a lusty cry.

"Oh!"

"It's a boy!" Bethan shouted.

"God be thanked! Ah, Emma, he's perfect! Well done, my girl."

"Wipe him off a bit and hand him to his mother. Yes," Maggie said.

Bethan followed her instructions on cutting the cord and handed the babe to Emma.

Emma unwrapped the blanket and fingered his toes, his hands. "He came from my body," she whispered. "How could it be? My boy." And she rested her lips on his forehead. Dawn had lightened the room, bathing mother and child in a golden glow.

"Emma, we must deliver the afterburden," Maggie said, interrupting Bethan's dreamlike state.

"A few more pushes. It will be uncomfortable, but

nothing like before," Bethan urged.

In a short time, the afterburden was delivered.

"Put it in the basin, Bethan. We must examine it to make sure nothing was left in her womb. At least that much I can do," she said dryly.

"If there are pieces missing, she will surely suffer from childbed fever. They fester inside."

Bethan nodded.

"Look it over carefully. Be thorough, turn it over. Don't be afraid to touch it with your hands." The bloody mass was like a creature from the deep sea, mysterious and pungent.

"Take care, for it could make the difference between life and death."

Bethan had mistakenly thought the challenge was over once the babe was born. She glanced at Emma.

"She's not listening. She's lost in the miracle of her babe."

"Then, despite any discomfort it causes the mother, you must massage her stomach, to rid the body of the blood and shrink the matrix."

"The matrix?" Bethan asked.

"The womb."

Bethan blushed at her ignorance.

After the afterburden was examined and deemed healthy, Maggie held the small of her back and closed her eyes.

"Are you well, Maggie?"

"Just tired."

"Why don't you go and sit down in the parlor?"

"No, I would see this to the finish. It will be my last delivery for a while, besides my own."

"Where is my Tom? Mother, will you fetch him?"

Emma's voice filled the room with joy.

Maggie waddled over to the side of the bed. "Emma, let Bethan take the babe for a moment. Grandmother, you fetch some warm water. We'll clean you up a bit and then you can show the babe off."

"Please hurry."

"I promise it won't take long."

Bethan and Mistress Evans soon had the new mother bathed, changed, and comfortable with a poultice of lavender and seaweed on her privities.

"Mistress Evans, why don't you get Emma something to eat, and a nice mug of ale. Tell Tom he can come in."

Indeed, Emma's mother looked as if a butterfly could knock her down, and no wonder.

She nodded and kissed her daughter's forehead. "I'm so proud of you, my Emma." Mother and daughter shared a moment of quiet intimacy. "You were very brave."

"Indeed," Maggie said. "One of the bravest new mothers I've ever seen."

Emma beamed.

"You're strong for a small lass," Maggie added, and clutched her stomach.

"What is it?" Bethan grasped her by the elbow.

"Nothing." Maggie waved her off. "You should know it's very common to have these cramps in the last days."

There was so much she didn't know. Was she ready to take the responsibility on?

Just then, Tom rushed in, face flushed. He embraced Emma and pulled back to view his son. "Oh, he's so small!"

He tentatively stroked the babe's cheek with a finger, and the babe turned toward him. "He knows me," he exclaimed. "Oh, Emma. Are you well? I heard you screaming. How I've hurt you."

"No, dear Tom. And anyway, it was worth it, for we have our boy now, don't we?"

As if in answer, the babe squawked.

Tom stepped back in alarm. "What's wrong with him?"

Emma laughed. "I expect he's hungry." With an instinct old as time, she bared her breast, and the babe latched on without further ado.

"Ouch!" She squealed.

The babe flung its chubby arms out and howled.

Bethan giggled.

Maggie chuckled. "Don't worry, lass. Your teats will toughen up."

"Holy God!" Emma said.

"I'll send your father in to see his first grandchild. Maggie held onto the door frame and slowly inhaled. "Where's your mother with the ale?"

Ian wheeled over to Maggie. "Sit down at once. You've overtaxed yourself."

"I *told* her to sit down," Bethan said. She sent the grandparents into the room again.

Ian stood up in the chair, holding onto the arm rests, knuckles white, arms shaking. "Damn these legs," he muttered.

Maggie sat in a chair by the fire.

"Sit down yourself, Bethan," Ian ordered. "You've had quite the night." He wheeled over to a table laden with comestibles. "Ale or tea?"

"Ale, please."

He fetched Maggie a plate heaped with sausages, bread, and cheese, and a mug of ale.

Bethan soon dug into her own meal. She'd not realized how hungry she was until then. After she finished, she made an effort to commit the birth to her memory. She grinned. She had delivered a child.

A short time later, Maggie fell asleep, plate resting on her belly. Ian retrieved it and lowered his voice to a whisper. "I think even my stubborn Maggie will admit she must now hand the reins over to you."

"Yes."

"She says your skill is intuitive."

Bethan took a sip of ale. "I have much to learn."

"She has faith in you. I am glad." He cocked his head toward Maggie. "For yon midwife will be putting her feet up until the child is born." He straightened in his chair, looking no less powerful for being in it.

She had no doubt. "During the birth, Maggie prayed to a 'Holy Sister.' Did she mean Mary? I didn't know she was Catholic."

"She's not."

He eyed the closed door of the birth room. "Maggie believes the spirit of Julian of Norwich aids her in her work."

"Julian of Norwich?"

"She was an anchoress in the fourteenth century, a nun who kept herself secluded in a cell to pray and seek God's guidance. She was besieged, or blessed, depending on your outlook, with visions." He glanced toward the door again. "I'll tell you more on the way home."

He wheeled over to the table and brought the pitcher of ale over to fill her glass. She nodded her thanks.

He tilted his head in his wife's direction. "She is exhausted, but will never admit it. I don't think it will be long." He grinned at her, and she had no problem seeing why the serious Maggie had fallen for him. The man teemed with energy.

He then wheeled over to the hearth to a blackened pot hanging over the fire. He stood, legs trembling, and filled a bowl with the fragrant stew.

"Thank you, Ian."

Just then, Maggie lifted her head and sniffed.

"Ah, you awaken. Here, I'll fetch you some."

To Bethan's great surprise, Maggie nodded. "I must admit I'm done in." As if to argue, her belly shifted and heaved. "Oh, hand it to me. I'm starving!"

With a comically frantic speed, he handed her a bowl.

"Eat, woman. Then I'll take you home." He ordered, in a tone brooking no argument.

Just then, the bedroom door opened, and Emma's parents emerged, beaming.

"Most beautiful boy ever born," Mistress Evans said, wiping tears from her ruddy face.

"I've got some brandy I've been saving for the event. Would ye share a bit with us?" The proud grandfather went straightaway to the cupboard.

"Of course," Ian said. "But then I must get her home." He took Maggie's empty bowl and refilled it.

She had color in her cheeks again and pointed with her empty spoon. "Mistress Evans, you look like you've been pulled through a knothole backward. Rest when you can, for your daughter and the babe will need you."

Mr. Evans pulled some fine goblets out of the

cupboard and dusted off a bottle.

"Would you care for some, Mistress Bethan?"

"Uh…yes. I've never tried it."

"A better brandy you'll never find. *French*," he whispered.

When they all had their glasses, Ian raised his.

"To your fine new grandson. May he grow fat as a summer lamb."

"Hear hear!"

Bethan took a tentative taste. The brandy burned down her gullet like liquid fire, then gushed through her body with warmth.

Mr. Evans raised his glass. "To Mistress Bethan and midwife Maggie, for bringing our bonny grandson into this world."

"Hear hear!"

"Bethan," Maggie said, holding her belly. "Last night you showed strength, endurance, and natural ability. My mothers are in good hands with you, and so am I."

"Hear hear!"

It was not just the brandy making Bethan glow from foot to toe.

Ian reached for Maggie's cloak. "Come, my lovely. We must get you to bed."

"Bethan here will return tomorrow to check on Emma and the baby." She looked at Bethan expectantly.

Bethan nodded.

Before long, the three of them set off for Maggie and Ian's cottage. Ian saw Maggie to bed and gave Bethan the herb poultice for Emma's privities. Bethan and Ian made their way to the Siren Inn through a dense fog. The sound of revelers at the Landgate alehouse echoed down the street, accompanied by the rumble of Ian's wheelchair.

"Take care on the cobbles, Bethan." He hummed along with the music.

"Do you mind?"

"Mind what?"

"Not being able to walk? God, I'm sorry. What a tactless thing to ask."

"Yes, of course I mind, as much as anyone would, I guess. But I know I wouldn't be alive if not for Maggie and the Holy Nun."

"I see."

He surveyed his legs thoughtfully. "The question I ask myself is not so much why I cannot walk, but why have I been given the gift of life. As impossible as it seems, I was the recipient of Julian of Norwich's grace."

They'd stopped in the middle of Siren Street. It was quiet, but for the creaking of the mermaid sign.

"You'll have heard the story of her sister, Sarah, how she was buried alive and found in time," Ian said.

"By you."

"Yes."

"We believe the spirit of Julian of Norwich helped Sarah survive her time underground."

"What?"

"I know, it sounds like an All Hallows' Eve tale. Maggie believes the Holy Nun is her mentor."

"I see."

So implausible, yet from what she knew of the practical Maggie, how could she not believe?

"Bethan, you would do well to respect the spirit of

the nun."

"I will be open to her presence."

"Sarah is forever altered and is becoming increasingly strange." He shivered. "She is no help to Maggie at this time."

They crossed the street and reached the door of the inn.

She tamped down the anxiety licking flames up her throat. "I will take care of Maggie as if she were my own sister."

He nodded. "I'll take leave of you now, Mistress Bethan. Congratulations. Rest your weary bones, for I expect my son or daughter will arrive soon." He grinned and made his way up the street, singing under his breath.

She paused before opening the door and let the memory of the evening's events encircle her. She might not be able to do anything for Elunid, but she could be of service to the good women of this town. Elation rose within her, sang through her with music, erasing her fatigue. She couldn't go inside, not just yet. If only she could share it with someone.

She heard the creak of the wagon wheels as if she'd summoned Henry. And why should she not share her joy? Her whole body hummed with life, her fingers tingled with the desire to touch him, to celebrate the wonders of her skin with the one man who made it come alive.

She threw off her cloak, took down her hair, and raised her arms, palms to the sky, enjoying the tiny droplets of moisture cooling her skin. But it did not cool the desire of wanting to touch someone. Henry. She let herself yearn.

Chapter Fifteen

Henry peered through the wisps of fog up Siren Street. The tall, proud figure of Bethan stood at the doorway. Her dark hair hung loose down her back, and she held her face up to the sky. He caught his breath at the sight of the white, translucent skin of her throat, the vulnerability and the strength of it. There was something different about her. She seemed brighter, more radiant. She lifted her palms to the sky, as if she could rise effortlessly into the air. She turned in his direction, dark blue eyes lit like a beacon. He lifted his hand to her without thought.

"George, could you do the next few houses for me, lad? You're ready to go it alone, don't you think?"

"Sure, Da!"

As he shortened the distance between them, the brilliance of her smile rammed his heart into his throat. He approached her, swallowed hard, and cleared it. She was so radiant it took all his courage to look upon her. "Good morning, Bethan." He bowed.

She closed the gap and grasped his arms. "Oh, Henry! I brought a new life into the world."

Her long fingers curled around his upper arms, and he breathed in her earthy, salty scent. She had a bead of moisture upon her cheek, and he longed to place his lips upon it, take her essence into himself.

"How extraordinary." His own voice echoed in his

ears.

Without warning, she drew him against her body and kissed him, her lips soft and cool on his, arms encircling him. He wrapped his arms around her, one hand on the back of her head, one at the small of her back. He breathed in her spirit, and her heartbeat entered him, filling his emptiness with her joy.

And then she broke loose. Had she come to her senses and realized her folly? No, for she searched his face, so close he could smell the scent of brandy on her breath.

"I wanted to share. I wanted…" Her eyes welled with tears.

"You wanted?"

"I want to share with *you*." She kissed him again, slowly.

He ran his hands down the curve of her hips. Then she released him, a question in her eyes.

He glanced to where George worked. All was well there. "Yes. Share with me, Bethan." He took her arm and led her to the garden behind the inn, motioned for her to sit on the bench against the garden wall. He took her hands, kissed her again while he had the chance. Her lips were soft as the rose petals overhanging the arbor.

"It was exhilarating, terrifying. I've never felt so alive!"

He nodded.

"There's so much I don't know, and soon Maggie will be having her child, and it will be up to me to deliver it safely."

He smoothed the crease of worry from her forehead.

She brightened again. "But I'm meant to do this, I'm certain."

How brave she was. "You will do it, Bethan. You will learn and grow in skill. You are a giver of life, for you have surely given me mine." He would tell her the secrets of his heart while he had the chance.

"Yours?" She cocked her head, silken hair falling over one shoulder. She gazed down at his mouth, and he stroked her cheek.

She met his gaze again. "Very forward of me to kiss you. But it seemed right."

"Yes." He kissed her again, fingers trailing along her slender neck, gratified to feel the tiny shivers coursing through her. He longed to traverse the contours of her breasts, but he might frighten her away.

"Da!"

What he wouldn't give to spend every early morning basking in her light.

Her sigh of regret did much to cheer him, despite his reluctance to break their embrace.

He stroked her cheek. "I'm sorry, but I must return to work."

He was afraid the mention of his occupation would make her recoil, but to his surprise she smiled, making his heart pound in his throat again.

"Thank you for sharing my joy, Henry."

"I would share it every day, like this." And hear his name spoken with such tenderness.

He offered up his best bow, one he might give to the queen, for she was his queen. He kissed her hand, fingers lingering on the soft skin, turned it over, kissed her palm. He turned and walked away. If he looked back, would she be watching him?

****

She viewed him until he disappeared, skin burning from his touch, the feel of his eyes dark upon her, and the soft, unfamiliar brush of his beard upon her face, the softness of his lips on hers. She'd never known a man's lips could be so soft, yet so strong.

She felt a jolt of recognition, then laughed. She cared not a whit about his occupation, not when he could make her glow all over.

The back door squeaked open, and Lena stood, a shawl wrapped around her shoulders.

"Bethan?"

She rose and spent an inordinate amount of time brushing herself off.

"You're so flushed, *Liebchen*. The air is cool still. Ah." She chuckled. "I hear the night wagon going up the street."

Bethan shrugged and grinned. Why try to deny her feelings for Henry, especially to Lena?

"Come, Bethan. You must be tired. So you are a midwife now. I am happy for you. Come in and have some pottage with fresh cream and sugar. And toast. I checked on your sister. She's still asleep."

Lena soon had her settled in front of the fire. Who knew how delicious plain oatmeal could be?

"You must tell me all about young Emma's trials."

They spent a congenial time by the fire, and when Lena rose to tend to her babe, Bethan leaned her head back in the chair and closed her eyes. His lips, the hard feel of his body against hers. She wanted more of him. Her desire shocked her with its intensity.

Much as she tried to block the memory from her mind, she couldn't: his naked body against hers, and the sight of him, skin glistening, his member stiff against the tangle of dark curls. Yearning surged heat through her center, and for a moment, she imagined herself entwined with him.

Elunid plopped into the seat beside her.

Bethan glanced at her, dreams of Henry fading. "Good morrow, Sister."

Her twin sniffed, nose in the air like a hound. "You've lust all over you."

"I beg your pardon."

Of all the mornings for her sister to notice the world around her. She took a measured breath.

Elunid surveyed her face as if she were a subject for her needlework. "Swollen lips, flushed cheeks. Hair in disarray."

Bethan smoothed her hair.

Elunid placed cold fingers upon her arm. "You needn't hide it from me, Sister. There's no shame in it. If yon Hephaestus warms your blood, so be it..."

Bethan sputtered, prepared to dress her down, but why bother? He *did* remind her of Hephaestus.

Elunid stared into the fire, humming a song Bethan had heard George sing the day before.

Suddenly the events of the night caught up with her, and her eyes grew heavy. "Elunid, I must have a lie down. Fetch me if you need to."

"Why would I need you?"

She was too exhausted to puzzle over the changing weather of her sister's mind.

Chapter Sixteen

Later that afternoon, Bethan awakened refreshed and entered the common area to find a crowd had gathered in her absence. Lena appeared from the kitchen carrying a tray laden with mollusks.

"Oh Lena! I'm so sorry. Here, let me take it."

"*Ach*! You needed your rest, and look all the better for it." She cocked her head toward Elunid, who sat at a table conversing gaily with Widow Jenkins. "She is well today, *ja*?"

"Yes, but it won't last."

She shoved Bethan gently toward her twin. "You've been given a gift. Go. Enjoy the moment." She sniffed. "I wish I'd enjoyed every minute with my Josef."

Bethan hugged her. "Thank you, Lena. I'll work hard for you today."

When she stood by the table next to Elunid, Widow Jenkins squealed and put her gnarly hand on her skinny chest. "Damn! Gave me a shock, you did. Look at the two of you together, looking so alike."

At rare times like these, Bethan had the sensation of looking at herself in a mirror.

"Look at that," the chandler said. "The touched one looks just like young Bethan."

"Her name is Elunid," Bethan said, putting her hand on her arm. "And I can tell you, we caused our

116

fair share of mischief in our younger days."

"Aye, Mother often said we raised her bile."

"And now I hear ye're a fair good midwife, young Bethan."

A rush of excitement filled her at being so named.

"I'm not sure it's right, you being a virgin, and seeing the tail end of a man's swiving," Widow Jenkins bellowed.

All present turned their heads. Unbidden, the image of Henry's bare chest appeared. Bethan reddened. "Mrs. Jenkins!" How was it old women could say anything and get away with it?

Elunid placed her hand atop the widow's gnarled one. "She may be young, but she's skilled beyond her years."

The old woman patted her hand. "If ye say so, dearie."

Could it be that Ian's medicine had cured her sister? Just as quickly, she rebuked herself for the foolish thought.

"Don't stand there gawping like a fish, fetch me some ale." The widow squawked.

At that moment, a group of sailors fresh off the boat wound their way in, landing at a table with a thunk.

"I must get to work," Bethan said. "Sister, I'm bringing you out a plate."

"Ye need fattening up, girl."

"I agree." Bethan grinned.

She took the sailors' orders: ale of course, and enough food to feed a light brigade.

She headed toward the bar, her eye still on Elunid. Suddenly, something hit her in the stomach, knocking the breath out of her.

"Oof," she grunted, knees buckling. She was dimly aware of liquid splashing on her arms.

"Oh God!" Henry put his arm around her. "I'm so sorry, Bethan. I couldn't see."

She slowly straightened. He helped her to a chair.

"I'm an oaf," he said. "I had the tray heaped high, and I turned my head, listening to Lena."

"No," she gasped. "I'm fine. I wasn't looking either."

He still had his hand upon her back and peered at her, concern creasing his forehead.

Mayhap she should feign ill health often, in order to be the subject of his care! But it wasn't her way.

He smiled, and she caught her breath. Something different about him… "Your beard!"

He had shaved it off. She let her fingers enjoy the square, smooth line of his jaw, the strong cheek bones.

"Do you approve?"

"Yes, of course."

"I did it for you, Bethan. Are you sure you're not hurt?"

"Yes, I'm sturdy as a barge, as Mother used to say."

He threw back his head and laughed. "A barge? Not how I'd describe you." He lifted her chin. "Someday, Bethan, I will make sure you know how beautiful you are."

"Henry, my kippers, man!"

"Hold on, James. You won't starve to death in a minute's time."

"I was fetching some ale for the sailors and Widow Jenkins. She's in rare form tonight, as is Elunid.

Where's George?"

"He had a sore throat, so I sent him to bed with licorice root tea."

"Elunid will be missing him."

He nodded.

"Everyone has been going on and on about how alike Elunid and I look."

"No, Bethan. I would never mistake you for your sister."

"How so?"

The path of his dark eyes sent a shaft of heat from her head to her toes.

"Girl, where's my ale?" one of the sailors yelled.

Henry shot him a dirty look. "Disrespectful lout."

"No harm done," Bethan said.

"Aye, save your canoodling for after hours, ye lovesick cows," Widow Jenkins hollered.

Bethan didn't heed the uproarious laughter that followed. What would it feel like to kiss the spot above his temple where one black curl fell?

His dark eyes glowed on her skin, as if he'd stripped off all her clothes. "Widow Jenkins is right. Would you care to *canoodle* later?"

She wasn't sure what it meant, but she'd be silly to deny herself the pleasure. Nevertheless she replied, "We'll see." She walked away and glanced over her shoulder, gratified to hear him groan.

Chapter Seventeen

Bethan had just sent Lena to rest in her private quarters when the door opened and a young man strode in. He was slightly built, but with a wiry strength about him, curly blond hair, and brown eyes. He glanced at the twins, eyes widening slightly. He settled himself in the corner table.

Widow Jenkins put her hand in front of her mouth. "Riding officer for customs. I haven't seen his face before."

"He looks bleary-eyed enough to have been up all night and all day too."

He took off his hat, dust falling upon the table. He leaned back in his chair and closed his eyes, then opened them just as quickly, eyes keen on the crowd.

Elunid sniffed. "I can smell his horse from here."

"There are worse smells than horse," Bethan said.

"Your shite monger? In the kitchen, fries fish, shovels shite. Versatile and quite right."

Widow Jenkins laughed.

"That's enough, Ellie."

"Dearie me," Elunid whispered to the widow. "She only calls me Ellie when she's vexed." She pointed one long index finger toward Henry, who'd come out of the kitchen to deposit a bowl of oyster stew in front of the chandler. One brow rose in provocation. "Quite right."

Bethan shrugged. Nothing would spoil her mood

tonight. She approached the table where the officer sat.

"You look like you could use a good meal and a glass of ale."

"Right enough, miss." He smiled and sat upright, rubbed his face with the palm of his hand.

"We've fresh chowder and bread right out of the oven."

"Sounds like heaven. Yes, please." He smiled, a dimple appearing in his chin.

The sounds of the crowd had lessened with the appearance of the riding officer, and an air of caution replaced the raucous mood. Instead of the usual friendly curiosity at sight of a stranger, several people kept darting glances at the young man.

It was a rare person in town who didn't have some part in smuggling one way or another. It was the riding officer's job to ride all night along the coast and prowl about town, recording bits of gossip, and apprehending anyone they discovered had been smuggling wool.

Hardly seemed fair to him, Bethan thought. He was only trying to get a good meal and a rest. And he was respectful and polite, which was more than she could say about some of the clientele tonight.

She promptly returned with the food. "Are you far from home?"

"Yes, miss. I come from a village outside of York."

"Ah. I stopped there on my way here."

"Where are you from?"

"Llandudno, Wales."

His bleached eyebrows rose at the strange roof of the mouth clicking sound she made when pronouncing the double "L."

The hours flew by as they served the good people

of King's Harbour. But it didn't feel like work, not with Henry there. She kept her eye on Elunid, who still chatted with Widow Jenkins. She grinned. What an unlikely pair they were.

Henry passed by then and whispered in her ear. "It does my heart good to see you smile, Bethan." His warm breath smelled of ale and apples.

She marveled anew at the smooth skin of his face. It made him seem stronger and emphasized the depths of his eyes, lit with promise and mystery.

The air cooled suddenly as the door opened, and Freddy walked in with a rough-looking sailor at his side.

"Ah, there's our fierce Amazon." Freddy rubbed his jaw, where a bruise bloomed.

Freddy's companion sported the hat and breeches common to a sailor but wore a large cross on a long chain.

His gaze writhed up her body. "Aye, lad. I see what ye mean."

As he loomed closer, the stench of rotten fish, sour sweat, and bitter tobacco rose from him in nauseating waves.

Without turning his head, he poked Freddy in the arm.

"Ow!"

"Where's the twin?"

Freddy searched the room. "There she is, Parson."

The man's strange lizard eyes hovered over the two of them, back and forth. "I see what ye mean! Been at sea for half a year, and God has blessed me with this vision, this miracle of double pulchritude. Zounds, they're mirror images!" He wheezed, spitting a glob of yellow mucus on the floor. "Good evening, my Godsends!"

"Surely and I'm not drunk yet." He gave Freddy a shove. "Fetch me some ale."

Bethan went over to where Elunid sat and put her arm around her. She'd grown stiff, and a subterranean growl rose from the back of her throat.

"God has brought me to you for a reason." He took the mug Freddy gave him, gulped it down, and when he exhaled with pleasure, the odor of rotten teeth filled her nostrils.

Bethan fought the urge to retch and rose to her full height. Despite what Mother said, towering over most men had its advantages. "What do you want?" She had to shout above the din of a heated game of chance.

"I require nothing but to feast my eyes upon the two of you, Godsend."

"You'll stop calling me that."

"And to have backbone as well? What have I done to deserve the blessings of the Almighty? Majestic breasts, legs I could climb all night…"

Widow Jenkins slammed her mug on the table and stood up. 'Get thee away, ill wind!"

He backed away in mock alarm. Bits of fabric sloughed off his coat. "Ooh, it's frightened I am of you, old nag."

"Leave her alone," Bethan said.

Widow Jenkins cackled. "You think he scares me, lass? I've coughed up worse than the likes of him."

The parson continued his perusal of their bosoms and licked his lips. He grabbed Freddy's coat. "Imagine how much…"

"What is it you want, piss breath?" Widow Jenkins

yelled.

The crowd roared.

"Shut yer gob, ye wrinkled old doxy."

Bethan restrained the old woman as she lunged forward, skinny arms flailing.

"Now see here. You'll not address her so."

When Elunid stood up to join Bethan in defense, the parson drew in his breath. "Cor. Imagine how much they'd fetch, the two of them. Praise the Almighty!"

Before Bethan could restrain her, Elunid poked him in the shoulder. Fibers of his coat came off in her hand. "Why are you called 'parson'?"

"Now, there's an inspiring story. I minister to the needs of mankind, wherever I might go, as God has asked me to do."

Elunid sniffed. "You carry the stench of Satan."

The crowd gasped.

He raised his hand, as if to slap her, then shook his head. Greasy strands of gray hair flopped in his eyes. "No, I can see you need saving."

"Brimstone," Elunid murmured in a strange monotone. "The sweat of suffering. Despair."

Bethan put a hand on her shoulder. "Ellie, stop."

She continued, "I'll wager you've spoken to the Dark One yourself."

He looked around, grinning. "Crazy, she is." He grabbed his crotch. "I've got something to cure you."

Elunid grew still. "Reminds me of…" She shook her head. "No."

"Ellie. Come along with me."

It was no use. When she grew stiff like this, she couldn't be reached.

Elunid circled the man and sniffed, eyeing him like

a piece of offal left steaming on the ground. "Filth like you are the devil's breeding ground."

"Here she goes again," someone in the crowd whispered.

Elunid sniffed again. "I smell animal. Sheep."

"I'm warning you, girl. Shut yer maw." He squinted with malevolence.

Freddy pulled at his sleeve. "Let's go, Parson."

"Yes," Bethan said. "Leave."

"I'll not be scared away by a woman."

Elunid's hair had fallen from her cap and hung over one eye. "Fetches a good price in Calais, yes? But that's the least of your sins."

From the corner of her eye, Bethan saw the riding officer slip out the door.

The parson grabbed Elunid and shook her, once. "See what you've done, you stupid bitch?"

"Get your filthy, whoring hands off her now." Bethan grabbed him by the shoulders.

He let go of Elunid and broke Bethan's grasp, grabbed her by the chin, thumbs, fingers digging into her skin, foul breath blistering her face.

Chapter Eighteen

Henry had been outside unloading goods from a wagon. He entered the crowded room to see a filthy sailor with his hands on Bethan.

He would have plowed through the gates of hell, let alone sailors, to get to her through the thick of the crowd. "Get out now, or you'll find your guts in your mouth." He grabbed the man by the shoulders, shook him hard.

"It's not your affair," he hissed, pulling out a knife.

"I warned you." Henry pulled his arm back and hit the man with such force, he slammed against the wall and dropped to the ground.

The parson got back on his feet with Freddy's help and spit out two rotten teeth and a mouthful of blood and saliva. He grinned, lips smeared with blood, eyes on the twins. "Oh aye. I'll minister to you."

"Not had enough?" Henry advanced, fists clenched. "Get out."

He signaled for two burly local lads to follow them out, then turned to the women. "Did he hurt either one of you? I'm sorry. I was out back, unloading goods."

Bethan had her arm around Elunid. "I need to get her to her room. She needs her..." She stared defiantly at the crowd gathered.

Henry turned on them. "What in the hell is the matter with you people? Could you not have come to the defense of one of your own, instead of staring like it was a show put on for your benefit? You should be ashamed of yourself." His deep voice echoed across the silent room.

The chandler muttered, "It's just that she's so fierce, and watching the two of them, together, looking so alike, it was mesmerizing."

"The Parson's not one to trifle with," one of the sailors said.

"You bloody cowards!"

He forced himself to breathe in and out, slow and steady.

"Sometimes the prospect of watching someone else's troubles overpowers the impulse to stick up for one's own," Bethan whispered.

"You never answered me. Did the bastard hurt you?"

She met his gaze. "I'm fine. I wish Elunid was."

He put a hand upon her cheek. "You don't have to do this alone anymore."

"You don't know what you're saying."

"I would do anything to ease your burden, Bethan." What could he do to convince her?

She nodded, not arguing with him for once.

"Your knuckles are bleeding." She took the handkerchief from her apron pocket and pressed it on the injury. His other hand rose of its own volition and covered hers.

"I smell him still. Smoke," Elunid spoke woodenly and shivered.

Widow Jenkins, looking the worse for wear, took Elunid's other arm. "He's gone now, dearie, and we're well rid of him."

"She's too far gone to hear you," Bethan said as they helped Elunid to her bedroom.

Widow Jenkins continued. "Ye've made an enemy today, you and your sister both. The customs officer heard every word she said. They're wool smugglers, ye see, and you can bet he's on their trail now. They'll blame you if they're caught. Before they hang, that is."

****

Henry waited outside the door for Bethan. He would have a word with her before they resumed working. He could hear her struggling with Elunid. Damn decency! She needed help. He had his hand on the door, when Lena bustled up the hallway.

"What's happened?"

He quickly filled her in, and she rushed to help Bethan. He returned to the main room. The crowd had died down, and he busied himself by cleaning up.

His fierce Bethan. Yes, she was his. He relished the pain in his hand. Sinking his fist into the bastard's face had been so satisfying. She would have endangered her own life for her sister, had in fact protected George a few months ago, towering over the sailors who'd made sport at his expense. Her fierceness had roused him then, and roused him now. What would it be like to call such a woman his? To be the recipient of her fierce love and protection of his heart?

Eventually he noticed the mood of the room had changed, and snatches of conversation brought his reverie up short.

"All we need around here is a customs officer nosing into our business. A man's got a right to make a living, doesn't he?"

"So a man needs to do a bit of business to keep his

children fed. Shouldn't be a crime."

"Best keep your mouth shut. Ye never know who might be spying."

Bethan emerged from the private quarters. The night had taken its toll on her. He fetched her a bit of brandy to put the color back in her cheeks. She took a sip and closed her eyes, then opened them again, pulled her shoulders back resolutely. Nodded. She set to work picking up dirty dishes, weaving gracefully around the crowd, smiling at one person, squeezing the shoulder of the next. A wisp of hair had come out of her cap to rest in the hollow between her breasts. How he would love to take his rest there after a day's work.

He approached her. "How is your sister?"

She shook her head, and his heart clenched at the anguished look in her eyes. "She's gone inside herself again, and will not stop shaking. I have…"

"What?"

"I've lost her again."

He took the wisp of hair between his fingers with great care, tucked it behind her ear, laid his palm upon her flushed cheek. "I'm sorry."

"When I get a glimpse of her as she used to be, and then lose her again, it's as if she's died." She swiped a tear from her eyes, pulled her shoulders back, and stepped away from him. "It's my life," she said with a hint of defiance, as if to say, is that the life you want?

"I'd like nothing more than to share the joys and the sorrows of life with you, Bethan."

She turned away from him. "Why would you want to saddle yourself with me? When you take me, you take my sister."

She didn't know the depths of his love for her yet.

Chapter Nineteen

The glum mood of the inn transformed when the Wandering Wastrels sallied in, their leader Reginald at the forefront. He wore a bright aqua waistcoat and underneath it a gold vest. On his head perched a tricorn hat dressed with a peacock feather. He'd like to dismiss the man and call him a dandy, but despite the fancy clothes, there lurked a pirate's allure, which, as always, seemed to appeal to the ladies, young and old.

"Why the long faces, my friends?" The dandy took off his hat and bowed. "It's a most beautiful night, the moon out and glowing like the face of a woman I've loved well."

The women, including Widow Jenkins, tittered and gawped at him, except for Bethan.

Reginald turned to Bethan. "Mistress Owen!"

Bethan stopped her work and smiled, her skin blooming like a ripe apricot and just as soft when he'd touched it.

Then the songstress Charlotte swept up beside Reginald. Some might find her fetching, with her face made up like a doxy's, and her bosom displayed for all to see. She *was* beautiful, but with a brittle kind of beauty, much like a china doll would break if you hugged it too hard. She took Reggie's arm, her eyes shooting daggers at Bethan, who'd resumed clearing tables, a small smile playing upon her face.

Mortimer the drummer skulked through the door, sporting a pumpkin-colored waistcoat and breeches, a snare drum tied with a rope around his neck, his suit pumpkin-colored. He held the drumsticks pointed like daggers.

Reginald stopped in front of Widow Jenkins, who was well into her cups by now.

"My beauty, why the scowl upon your lovely face?" He grabbed her hand and kissed it.

She giggled. "An ill wind blew in, but it's gone now." She pulled her hand away. "Get thee away from me, knave! I'm too old for your foolishness."

Lena came out of the kitchen, plump cheeks red from cooking. She stopped shortly upon seeing Reggie, and a smile lit her face. Oh. He'd better keep an eye on that.

Just then, Bethan walked by, struggling under a heavy tray of dishes. He made his way over, but damn Reggie beat him to it.

"What's this? Let me carry that for you, my queen."

"I have it."

"No, I insist." He took it from her, holding it high above his head. "If you were my queen, you'd not have to lift a finger."

"I'm nobody's queen." She scowled at him, but her eyes shone.

"You *could* be my queen." Reggie winked.

Like hell she could!

"Ah, Lena. Tell me. Are you as tasty as your dishes?"

She giggled and slapped his chest. "*Ach, Dummkopf!*"

"You wound me, lady!"

Enough of this nonsense. He shoved by with his empty tray.

"Oh, good evening, Henry."

"Yes, uh…well."

The fool returned to Bethan's side. "What else may I do for you, my queen?" He took her hand and kissed it.

"Enough!" He'd had no intention of growling, but the sight of the scoundrel's lips on her skin… "Reggie, don't you have a song to sing?" Before he knew it, he was nose-to-nose with him.

Reggie backed away. "What ails you, man?"

Bethan put her hand over her mouth. Minx!

She glanced at his fisted hands. "He means no harm, Henry."

He forced himself to walk away and busy himself behind the counter. Could Bethan be so shallow as to really care for the lout? Was *Reggie's* occupation more…palatable? Perhaps she did find him loathsome after all; although he thought she'd overcome her revulsion of his job, mayhap it still bothered her.

For the first time since George was a baby, he let himself think of the positive aspects of his other life. In another life, he had dressed like an aristocrat, stood in ballrooms, received visitors, done what every man in his position would do to maintain his standing in society.

He would say something charming, stay by her side and hand her a glass of champagne, watch her eyes light up at the bubbles. Later, he would take the champagne glass from her hands, and sweep her away in a dance. How surprised she would be to see him in that light. But he was no longer that man.

"Why the scowl, old friend?" Zounds, how did Ian manage to sneak up on him, even in the wheeled chair?

He'd not realized he still stared at Bethan, who attended a table of very drunken seaman.

"Ah," Ian rumbled.

"Never mind," Henry snapped.

"Oh ho."

Henry turned, put his hand on the wheelchair's handle. He bent toward Ian's ear. "I don't know where I stand with her."

"Are you daft, man? Do you not see how she looks at you?"

"I fear she may carry a torch for yon Reggie."

"Don't be a fool, Henry. He is like marzipan, attractive, but insubstantial. A woman can't survive on marzipan. Can you blame her for wanting some levity, with the weight of her sister always on her shoulders? She is much like my Maggie, hard-working, always putting the needs of others before her own. Mayhap you should provide Bethan with some amusement?"

His friend had a point. The conversation appeared to be at an end, for Ian stared at Maggie, who had waddled in ahead of him and sunk into a chair at a table, quickly attended to by Bethan.

"It's awfully late for you to be out, isn't it?"

"Yes, but she was hungry, and she's eaten all the food in the house. She is magnificent, my queen of fecundity, tender and fierce by turns. I never know these days which she will be. Invigorating!" Without further ado, he wheeled his way to her, greeting Bethan heartily.

Bethan's shiny chestnut hair had come out of her

cap again. If he could, he would trace the slender lines of her neck, tuck the hair into her cap so he could kiss the back of her neck, skim his lips over her downy skin to see her goosebumps rise. He would kiss each bare shoulder, trail his lips down one slender arm, revel in her shiver. Watch the landscape of her smooth skin change to bumps of arousal.

Bethan suddenly turned to gaze at him, a shocked look on her face. Mayhap his face had revealed his passion? He grinned, rewarded when she grinned back. Yes, he would plan to show Bethan another side of him, make sure she knew she was his, and his alone.

****

Later, Henry left the inn through the back door opening to the garden and an alleyway. In the far corner, a woman stood against the wall, the man leaning in to kiss her, arms bracing either side of her. Not an uncommon sight this time of night. The man, or boy, as it turned out, pulled his head away and put his hands upon her breasts, whereupon she giggled. Wasn't that Freddy? And he'd know that giggle anywhere—Isadora.

He shook his head. The girl was no concern of his, but he would not have her innocence sullied by such a lout. He whistled, stared pointedly in their direction. They broke apart.

"What do you want, man?" Freddy said.

"Isadora, get ye home before I take you home myself. You have no business with the likes of him."

She scowled at him, the little chit.

"I'll escort you home." Did she not have a bit of sense?

She blew a kiss at Freddy and stomped ahead of

Henry. When he saw her safely home, he set off toward the Landgate. George had been sleeping soundly when he left, would hopefully sleep his ague away. Nevertheless, he quickened his pace; he didn't like to leave him alone when he was sick.

Life was like the clouds over the Channel. They could blow away with the wind or gather in anger for a storm. One day he put his arm around his wife, looked upon his newborn son, counting the perfect toes and perfect fingers, and in the blink of an eye, he stood over her grave. Memories swept over him. Though the marriage had been arranged, he had loved her in his fashion and missed her still. But he would not waste time in living now he had found his Bethan.

He crept into the cottage, relieved to find George sprawled above the covers in front of the fire, one arm above his head, his sturdy legs akimbo. He'd gotten so big, his boy. He was eleven now, a well-built lad. Though he could not yet read, he could read people better than most adults, and had a way with animals and troubled souls like Elunid.

As always, his thoughts returned to Bethan, the look upon her face when she'd awakened in his arms to see his nakedness: shock, wonder, arousal. He hardened at the memory. There was a time when no woman could have distracted him from the care of his son. He laid his hand on the boy's forehead. His cheeks were flushed and warm, but nothing to be concerned about.

He stretched his back, feeling the pull of sore muscles. It had been a busy night. How tired Bethan must be, after barely sleeping the night before, then working all night at the inn. He dressed for bed, imagining her slender fingers pulling the linen shirt over his head, fingertips grazing his sides. His stomach muscles tensed, sending pulsing beats to his member.

She would slowly unlace his breeches, her lips upturned with mischief. Oh God. She would pull his breeches down, hands skimming his leg to cup one calf muscle in her hand, her silken hair brushing against his hard member. He'd lift her to her feet, carry her to the bed, and say with his body what he could not articulate in words. Then, when they had reached their joy, he'd watch her sleep with pride of possession.

What manner of torture was this? How could he convince her he would protect her, care for her and her sister both? For suddenly, life as it was, was not enough.

Chapter Twenty

Dear Lord, her feet ached. Bethan sat slumped at the table with a mug of ale in her hands, and eyed the filthy floor. She'd told Lena and Sabine to go to bed. Only one customer, old man Wyeth, remained, and he was so far in his cups he'd sleep until noon.

What a night. First, the joy of holding a real conversation with her sister, then the appearance of the skin-crawling "Parson," Elunid's foolish antagonizing of the man, and Henry's fierce defense. What would it be like to let down her guard, let Henry take care of her, love her?

A bitter laugh escaped her lips, causing old Wyeth to roll over. As if any man would chain himself to her and her sister both. He didn't know what he was getting into, what she and Elunid had endured. She could not bear it if he abandoned her, as her mother did. And her father, through no fault of his own.

Still…denying her feelings for him was like holding back high tide. She allowed herself the momentary luxury of thinking about her needs, what she yearned for: the feel of his strong arms against her, his warmth, protection, and passion. Why torture herself with what couldn't be? For no one who'd loved her had stayed.

She stood, besieged by a restlessness she'd not experienced before, a longing for something she didn't understand. Mayhap a bit more hard labor would calm her.

By the time she finished cleaning, she was good and tired and stepped outside for some air. She let the cool mist of the sea bathe her work-warm face. Footsteps echoed down Siren Street, and in the distance by the docks, the bright moon revealed a figure running with a bundle, bee skep over its head.

She'd heard about smugglers using the manmade bee hives to disguise their identity while in the act of transporting goods, but had never seen it. The moon reflected on something shiny. She'd seen that belt buckle before. Freddy.

She stepped inside before she was seen, heart pounding. Elunid had already endangered them all with her behavior, but she was no doubt right about the wool smuggling.

A wave of darkness suddenly enveloped her, like being swept into a dark storm cloud. She shivered. Elunid. She rushed down the hallway to her sister's room. Her eyes adjusted to the dim light as she approached the bed.

Elunid lay stiff as a corpse, the bedcovers pulled up to her eyes. Her long white arms lay outside the covers at her sides, fists clenched.

"Elunid?"

The covers lowered to her chin. "Sister?"

"How are you?" She had given her a double dose of Ian's medicine. It had not lasted long this time.

"Awake." Elunid's voice sounded disembodied, empty.

"Yes, evidently. Why do you not get up? Here, I'll help you." Her muscles ached with fatigue, but she forced herself to move.

"I cannot."

"What do you mean, you cannot?" She swallowed down her irritation.

Elunid's voice was hoarse, as if she'd been screaming all night. "They won't let me rise."

"Who won't?"

"Shit wit. The same, as I've told you more times than a whore beds a sailor."

"I'm trying to help you, but I'm very tired." Her needs didn't matter, of course. She couldn't help the surge of anger and then the guilt passing over her.

"They are punishing me for enjoying the pleasures of this earthly world, and not toiling on their behalf, sewing, sewing, bleeding for them."

Bethan sat on the bed and covered Elunid's clenched fist with her hand. "You're freezing."

"Better to freeze than burn in hell."

No sense trying to talk her out of her darkness. She'd learned it was fruitless a long time ago. She tried to lift Elunid's fist, but it was stiff and unyielding.

"They said they were kind," Elunid rasped. "They would give me two more days, so I might finish my needlework before the sun came up. But if the sun goes down upon my imperfection, it will not rise again." The despair in her voice chilled Bethan to the bone.

She brushed Elunid's hair away from her eyes. "The sun will rise again, Ellie. It always does, always will."

There was nothing she could do about her twin's condition, and since it appeared she wasn't moving anywhere, at least mayhap she could get a few hours' sleep in her bed. Her legs threatened to give out on her as she fetched another blanket to put over Elunid's stiff form.

Elunid's dark blue eyes stood stark against the white sheets. "They are kind to let me have two more days. I can bide here awhile, think on how I could please them most."

"Elunid, you have only to fetch me when you are ready to get up. Perhaps after you work awhile tomorrow, I'll take you to the Shipwreck Hotel for tea in the afternoon. I've heard their dessert cart is outstanding. It won't take all day, just an hour."

The glimmer of interest in her eyes did much to buoy Bethan's spirit.

"They have all manner of treats. I'll use the coin I earned delivering the baby."

"No, I cannot risk it," Elunid said, her eyes resuming their glazed look.

Once in her sleeping quarters, Bethan undressed and slipped into the clean, smooth sheets. At least for a few hours she could escape into oblivious slumber, and if she happened to dream about a muscular man with warm brown eyes, it was certainly not of her doing.

Chapter Twenty-One

Bethan awoke in the early afternoon, feeling refreshed. She dressed, made a cup of tea, and went to Elunid's room.

Her twin sat in the straight-backed chair by the window, dark hair loose and falling over one shoulder. Her long fingers danced upon the fabric as she pulled a needle in and out of the cloth.

"You're up," Bethan said.

"I can still rise from bed on my own," Elunid said without lifting her head from her work. "I could not very well remain there, with Them nattering on about the day wasting away."

Bethan wasn't inclined to ask her to elaborate, so she perched on the bed and sipped her tea.

"Ellie, do you remember when we used to dress alike and confuse Mother and the townspeople?"

She glanced up from her work and smiled. Bethan caught her breath, for she was so beautiful when she smiled. Is it how she herself looked?

"Sister, what do you say we create a little mayhem today?"

"I have accomplished much, and they are pleased," Elunid said. "Mayhem? Oh yes, let's!" She carefully placed her needlework in a basket and rose to open the armoire. "Do you still have the peacock dress we made a few years ago? This one?" She pulled out a brilliant blue dress made of silk.

"Of course I do. It's a work of genius, Elunid. I still cannot believe you were able to sew it."

A dimple appeared in Elunid's cheek. She held the dress up to herself. On the bodice, two peacock heads nestled together, entwined, with many shades of blue and green. Their feathers continued on the overskirt, replete with eyes: an outer ring of mint grass green, bronze, then a robin egg blue, and in the center, a watchful indigo blue.

"We shall wear them, and the town will never be the same," Elunid declared.

"So beautiful," Bethan said. "A bit dressy, though."

Elunid put one slender arm on her hip. "When else will we get to wear them? We will never be as beautiful as we are now."

Bethan laughed. "Speak for yourself."

Excitement coursed through her, and she hurried to her room to dress, taking care with her hair, sweeping her heavy locks up on one side of her head, twisting it into a knot, letting tendrils fall on her neck.

Elunid arrived, and just like old times, had unknowingly fixed her hair the same way, except that she had twisted it on the opposite side of her head. They stood in front of the mirror. Elunid's eyes were clear as a brook and alight with mischief.

Bethan had forgotten the joy of dressing in something beautiful. The dress fit perfectly, the skirt flaring out at the bottom. The peacock blue brought out the color of her eyes, and the low-cut bodice displayed the smooth rounded swells of her breasts.

"*Chwaer*, even I can't tell us apart," Bethan murmured.

When they walked into the empty main room, Lena rose to her feet, eyes round as dinner plates. "Look at the two of you!"

The two women glanced at each other, and simultaneously said, "Hello, Lena. How do we look?"

"You are breathtaking. I cannot tell you apart." They giggled at Lena's perplexed face.

"Let's go," they said in unison and laughed.

She kissed both on the cheek and waved them off. "Go now, and tell me all about it when you return."

Before Bethan could push the door open, a lad of ten or so entered. Upon seeing them, he croaked, "oddzooks," and staggered backward, blushing a bright red.

"Good afternoon, sir," they chorused.

He opened his mouth wide enough to sail a clipper ship through.

They made their way carefully over the cobblestones. A fair amount of people strolled about in the fine weather, and greeted their appearance with a stunned silence, then excited conversations and pointing. The twins held hands and greeted the neighbors in unison.

Ed the butcher dropped the mutton leg he'd been wrapping. "Of all that's holy, I've never seen such a sight. Such beauties you are!"

"Thank you, kind sir." They curtsied.

"It's sorry I feel for all the young lads in town today. They'll never be the same."

"We'll see." They waved and continued on their way.

"It's like when we were children, isn't it?" Bethan hooked her arm with Elunid's. "When all we had to worry about was what we were having for tea."

Elunid nodded.

Martha, the baker's wife stood outside, fanning her face. "Bethan, Elunid!" She giggled. "Whichever one you are, don't you look lovely." She approached them and fingered the embroidery on Bethan's bodice. "Who did this lovely work?"

"I did." Bethan said.

"Elunid?"

"Is it?" They both said.

Martha shook her head. "Aye, it's double trouble you are. Your eyes sparkle with it." She turned at the sound of her daughter exiting the bakery. "Isadora!" She shook her head. "I haven't gotten a lick of work out of her today. She's so tired. I hope she isn't ill. "

"Maybe I am, Mother. Sick of you," she said under her breath.

"What did you say, chit? Where do you think you're going?"

Isadora turned for the first time, gave the girls a blank stare. "Hello," she muttered. Her gaze bounced between the two. "Why are you dressed up?"

"We're going to the Shipwreck Hotel for tea," Bethan said. "Care to join us?"

"Some of us have to work." Isadora scowled at her mother.

"You may go for a stroll with them after you get those tea cakes finished. Mayhap a walk will put some color in your cheeks."

Isadora nodded and returned to the shoppe without saying goodbye.

They said their goodbyes and continued downhill toward the Shipwreck Hotel.

"It would be good to have a friend our own age, wouldn't it? Mayhap Isadora was just out of sorts today."

"She's always out of sorts."

She was about to lecture her twin on the merits of kindness but decided otherwise.

A group of bedraggled seamen staggered up the hill. Upon seeing the two women, the one in front stopped short, causing his followers to run into his back. Over the chorus of cursing, he bellowed, "Neptune's ballocks, was I hit on the head and now I see double?"

"Me eyes is playin' tricks on me!" A tall man, reeking of gin, pushed the leader aside.

Not to be outdone, a portly gentleman popped his head out of the melee and approached the girls. "Can I touch ye, see if you're real?"

"No, you may not." Bethan held her skirts away from him and drew herself taller.

"Aye, they's tall, ain't they? Could wrap those legs around me anytime. See if one of them won't before the day's through."

Derisive snorts of laughter followed his statement. He sidled closer to Bethan, and eyed her up and down. Loud enough for the French to hear in Calais, he yelled, "Care to follow me down to the ship's hold, and hold this?" He put his hand on his bulge.

Elunid advanced on them, fist in the air. "Clear off, shit wit."

"Ooh now! Fierce, she is. Mayhap I'll take them both."

"Aye, for sure you got a way with women."

They'd circled the girls, and Bethan glanced at

Elunid to see her reaction. So far so good, but she didn't care for the turn this was taking.

Just then, Reginald broke through the crowd. "Now, see here…"

He stood in front of the men, wielding a knife.

They dispersed, and the tall one mumbled, "It was love we was after, not fighting."

"Best of luck with that, Sir Uggers," Reggie quipped. "Now, then." He took off his hat and bowed to the ladies. "I've been around the world, and I swear I've seen nothing as lovely as the two of you."

Bethan couldn't help admiring his grace and carefree attitude. Had she ever been so carefree?

He took Elunid's hand and kissed it, and she snatched it away. His eyes had gone dark as midnight.

At his puzzled look, Bethan hoped he didn't think her jealous when she said, "Elunid doesn't like to be touched."

"Ah. What about you, Mistress Bethan?"

She sputtered. What a question. "Oh dear, we're late for tea."

"Yes." Elunid took Bethan's arm.

"May I escort you? I'd not want you to encounter any more ruffians."

"We can take care of ourselves," Elunid said.

"I've no doubt, mistress, but I'd like to just the same."

"Shipwreck Hotel, then." Elunid took the lead.

"I have a proposition for you, ladies."

They turned to him as one.

"No, not that kind of a proposition. How would you like to join the Wandering Wastrels?"

Travelling the world with a ragtag gang of

minstrels. What fun! Then she remembered who she was.

"You'd cause quite a stir, especially if you could sing."

"Of course we can sing," they chimed.

"Lordy!" He laughed, showing perfect, white teeth.

"Aye, but nay, I cannot go, for I must sew," Elunid sang.

"She cannot go, for she must sew," the minstrel burst out in a loud baritone.

Elunid hid her smile behind her hand.

"Sounds like a fairly boring song, a song about sewing," Bethan said.

"What do you suggest we sing, my fair peacock?"

Bethan blushed. "I said I *could*, I didn't say I would. I've not sung in so long, I scarce remember any songs." She was lying, of course. She remembered the words to every song she'd ever heard.

"Why have you not sung?"

She glanced at Elunid, who'd encountered Widow Jenkins and basked in her cooing praise. "I've more pressing matters to attend to."

Reggie nodded. "I see. Can you not sing a song now and then in these moments of—quietude?"

"I cannot."

Nevertheless, he opened his mouth and began singing "Scarborough Fair," only the words...

"Are you going to swive me, my dear?
In a bed of parsley and thyme,
Remember me for one who swives well..."

Bethan gave into his tomfoolery, Elunid following suite.

Then Widow Jenkins descended on him, beating

him about the head and shoulders with her gnarled fists. "Why, ye should be ashamed of yourself, knave!" She yelled between wheezes. "Just like you youngsters to make sport of such a grand song."

Reginald cowered with mock fear, collapsed to one knee, and grabbed her hand. "I beg of you, my beauty, please forgive me."

The widow opened and shut her mouth, then barked with laughter. She shoved him with surprising strength. "I've more important things to do than listen to your nonsense." She smiled at the girls. "May you be doubly blessed this day, my girls." She hobbled down the street.

The three of them stood for a moment, until Bethan said, "I certainly hope I've such vigor when I'm her age."

Reginald grinned and tidied himself up. "Where were we? Oh yes, we were discussing the Wandering Wastrels, and how you'd like nothing more than to travel the world with us."

"We cannot," they said in unison.

"Then a song, please. 'She Moved Through the Fair'?"

She opened her mouth to sing, then shut it again. Why pretend she had a normal life? It would just remind her of what she'd given up when Elunid got sick. Besides, why enjoy something when it would be snatched away without warning? It made it all the more difficult when it happened, because this fine day would not last.

"No."

Reggie sighed. "As you wish, my queen."

They continued their descent toward the docks and

the Shipwreck Hotel; a crowd of onlookers followed them, eager for the spectacle, no doubt.

They crossed Market Street and passed the apothecary shoppe. Maggie stepped out, holding the door open for Ian to come through with his rolling chair.

"It's a miracle his contraption fits through the door," Reginald said. "Or yon Maggie."

Elunid giggled. Reggie stared at her, opened his mouth to say something, and closed it again.

Then he smiled and eyed Maggie again. "She's beautiful in a rather frightening mother bear way."

"Careful, she might hear you," Bethan warned.

"You're quite right. The last time I commented on his wife's beauty, I nearly got a fist down my throat."

"Oh dear," Elunid whispered.

As Maggie held the door open for her husband, they found he could not exit due to her immense belly.

Reginald rushed over. "Here, Mistress Pierce. Allow me." He held the door open for her, she nodded her thanks, and Ian wheeled himself out.

"A pair of peacocks," Ian exclaimed. "How magnificent you are!"

Maggie held her belly, which to Bethan's admittedly inexpert eye, looked as if it had dropped. "So alike you are today, exotic birds. Wherever did you get such dresses?"

"I made them," they both said.

"No, you don't mean it!"

"Aye!"

"You little minxes," Ian exclaimed." I cannot tell between the two of you. How extraordinary." His gaze rested upon Bethan's face. "Ah."

They shared a silent moment of communication, and Ian whispered, "I'm happy for it, Bethan."

Then he grasped Maggie's hand and sang.

"Come my beauty, sit upon my lap
Why is it so hard for you to love this chap?"

Maggie rolled her eyes. "You know I cannot sit on your lap. I'll break Henry's fine chair. And have you not sung enough today?" She had the harried look of a woman who'd been tested to her limit.

"I'm sorry, my love. As I can't walk, I sing to calm myself."

She squeezed his hand. "I'm the one who's sorry."

He kissed her. "You know I don't blame you for it, Maggie. I'm alive, and with you."

Bethan suddenly felt like an intruder.

"The man couldn't be more besotted," Reggie whispered. "And she must love him very much to tolerate his…eccentricities."

Much to Bethan's surprise, Elunid said, "Do you want a wife, Reginald?"

He laughed shortly, then turned to Elunid, mouth working soundlessly for a moment. "I desire love, I love desire. And as it turns out, I'm on an eternal search for a woman upon whose shoulders depends the rising of the sun."

Elunid started. "The sun…"

Bethan squeezed her hand in warning. "Oh my, Reginald. You don't ask for much, do you?"

"I've been all over the world and have never found her, so I can only surmise she doesn't exist."

"I'm hungry, husband," Maggie said.

They made their goodbyes and soon arrived at the inn.

Reginald bowed. "I must take my leave now, ladies. I pray you consider my offer to join our merry band."

Didn't he realize how impossible the offer was?

Just then, Charlotte exited the inn. "There you are, Reginald. I thought you were going to meet me here." She pouted. "I had to eat alone." She glanced at the twins. "Splendid dresses! Did you order them in London?"

"No, we've not been to London," Elunid said.

Charlotte smoothed down the front of her lavender dress. "I had this made in London." She peered up at them. "Where *did* you purchase them?"

Bethan sighed. If she didn't eat soon, she'd faint. And instinct told her the less Charlotte knew about them the better.

"I made them," Elunid said.

"Perhaps you can make one for me."

"No," Elunid said. "Only two in existence."

"I'll pay you handsomely."

She flicked her eyes dismissively over Charlotte's petite form. "I fear the dress would not flatter you."

Charlotte's overflowing bosom turned red as a stewed tomato.

"Come, Sister." She tried to ignore the look of utter venom in the woman's eyes.

Bethan took Elunid's arm. "Reginald, thank you for escorting us."

"A double pleasure for me," Reggie said.

Charlotte poked his arm. "You owe me an explanation, making me eat alone today."

Elunid shook her head as they watched the two head for the docks. "She's got the choking kind of love."

"I won't disagree with you, Sister. But why did you antagonize her? I'll never understand you, not if we live to be a hundred years old."

"Oh, I assure you I won't," Elunid said darkly as they entered the inn.

Chapter Twenty-Two

They entered the inn to the friendly clatter of a crowd enjoying their meal, and giggled nervously at the sudden silence and the sight of forks and knives in the air.

"Land sakes!" Mrs. Reynolds, the short and very rotund mistress of the inn put her hands to her cheeks. "What have we here? You are most heartily welcome, my sweet birds!"

She looked around her at the quiet room. "Now, don't let my food get cold!" She motioned for the girls to follow her to a table by the window. Bethan's stomach growled at the aroma of freshly baked bread and roasted chicken.

"Ye look fair starving." She snatched a plate of scones, clotted cream, and jam from the table next to them, much to the man's surprise. "Here's a bit to take the edge off."

Elunid took the seat with a view of the ocean. "It's so clear today; I swear I can see France." She generously buttered a scone, topped it with cream, and took a bite. She sighed loudly. Their fellow diners glanced up from their food, looking slightly scandalized.

"These scones, so light!"

"I agree. Delicious!"

A movement outside the open window interrupted

her reverie. Henry and George stood, close enough she could reach out and touch Henry if she desired. He wore a fine, gray waistcoat, sleeveless, with a blue necktie. A crisp, white linen shirt, rolled to the elbow, accentuated his brown, muscular forearms. *Oh yes, she did desire.*

His clean jaw brought out the fullness of his lips. A single black curl lay on his forehead, making her long to straighten it to watch it spring back again.

Young George was similarly attired. Henry smiled at him, and the sun lit his eyes, turning them to an autumn gold. He reached over and straightened the boy's necktie. "Now George. As a lad of eleven, it's important you learn the art of fine dining. Remember what we practiced?"

The boy grinned. "Aye, Da."

"Let's imagine I'm Lady Merry Cheeks."

Why would George ever need to know how to treat the aristocracy?

George giggled as Henry simpered and curtseyed. "Begging your pardon, Da. I'm so hungry."

"One moment, George. Let's imagine this fine lady."

Bethan giggled. Apparently this lady had a prominent bustle, for Henry, with not a care for who saw, stuck his backside out and pursed his lips as if he'd swallowed a green apple.

George dissolved in laughter, bending over and holding his stomach. "Da!"

As she watched the love shared between father and son, she felt as if her soul had taken wing, and she soared with the joy of it.

"Okay, young George. Let's imagine we all sit

down to dinner. What do you do?"

"Eat? I'm hungry, Da!"

"No, lad. You pull the chair out for the lady and help her into her seat."

A pause. When nothing happened, Henry squeaked, "I'm ready to be seated, sir."

George giggled, covered his mouth, and jumped to action, pulling out an imaginary chair.

"Night soil man's lost his mind," Mistress Reynolds said.

Still, Bethan couldn't take her eyes away from him.

Henry batted his eyes, fluttered his eyelashes, and took his time sitting down, then smoothed his imaginary dress, and fanned himself.

George laughed so hard he gasped for breath. "Oh Da! You're splitting my sides!"

"Push my chair in, if you please."

"There you go, madame," George said.

"My, my. Such a gentleman you are! You make my heart go pitter pat, you do. You may be seated now."

"Can we not sit for real, Da?"

Henry ruffled the boy's curly hair. "Are you ready to celebrate your birthday in style?"

He put his arm around the boy and opened the door, motioning for him to go in first.

Chapter Twenty-Three

Henry and George entered the inn, the homey scent of cakes enveloping them and making Henry's stomach growl. Mrs. Reynolds rushed over, plump and warm as the tea cakes she served. "Oh my, how handsome you two look."

Henry removed his tricorn hat and nodded. "Thank you."

Much to his amusement, George did the same.

"It's my birthday," he said.

"Well, a happy birthday to you, lad!" She enveloped him in a hug. "Must be the day for dressing up." She cocked her head toward the bay window.

Sweet Mary. He felt as if he'd fallen out of a tree and had the breath knocked out of him. There was an odd buzzing in his ears, like bees in a thicket. Her glossy chestnut hair swept up on her head showcased the radiance of her face. She met his gaze, and he reached into the twilight waters of her eyes. No matter the cost, he would do whatever it took to swim forever in those depths.

"Eek!"

He'd trodden upon poor Mrs. Reynold's toes. "I'm so sorry, mistress."

Had Bethan seen it? Of course she had. His neck itched with heat as she grinned behind her hand. Years of having manners drilled into him by his family and she'd turned him into a schoolboy. He was supposed to be amusing her, not making a dolt of himself.

Mrs. Reynolds led the way, limping a bit. "Follow me, gentlemen."

She led them to the table next to Bethan and Elunid, and the closer they got, the louder the buzzing in his ears.

George stopped in front of their table. "Good afternoon, ladies."

He managed it so gallantly, Henry didn't know whether to laugh or cry. Who was teaching whom about proper etiquette? He'd have to depend on George for etiquette, for he could only gaze at her face, the apricot tinge to her cheeks, winged brows upon her smooth forehead, the regal grace of her neck, those white shoulders.

George shook his shoulder. "Ahem!"

Pull yourself together, man. "Good afternoon. Elunid, Bethan."

"How is it you can tell the two of us apart?" She had a look about her, as if she'd like to kiss him.

It gave him courage. He'd never seen the dimple below her eye before, as often as he'd studied her face.

He took her hand and kissed it, his lips lingering on her knuckle. "I would always know it was you."

Chapter Twenty-Four

The pressure of his silken lips on her hand lingered long after he'd released it, and she tried to breathe; how awkward he must think her, to be so flustered by a man kissing her hand.

Mistress Reynolds tittered. "I've a grand idea! We shall put your two tables together."

"Excellent idea," Henry murmured, eyes dark with mystery, sending rivulets of chills down her spine.

Although she couldn't seem to break their gaze, Bethan felt the rush of air as a fresh tablecloth was put on the table, the clink of silverware as the table was laid, the absence of warmth as Henry released her fingers to sit down at the table opposite her.

"Oh, this is a party, Da!" George grinned, eyes bright as beacons.

"Happy Birthday, George." Elunid smiled brilliantly.

"Thank you, Elunid." He blushed, peeking at her through lowered lashes. "You're so bright today, like a rainbow."

"A double rainbow." Elunid laughed.

George said, "You are happy today. And it makes me happy too."

"It is a good day," Elunid said.

A rare day, fleeting, and meant to be cherished.

"My son has outshone me in manners and charm

today." He grasped her hand across the table. "I was waiting for the right words to celebrate your beauty, but he has beaten me to it." His eyes swept over her. "Not everyone could outshine a peacock, but you do."

"I…" And then her stomach growled.

George giggled. "You sound like an angry bear, Miss Bethan!"

"It was me," Henry said.

Very game of him, but he fooled no one.

Fortunately, Mistress Reynolds rolled the tea cart laden with tea sandwiches, baked chicken, fresh oysters. The table grew quiet as all enjoyed a most delicious meal.

Clearly Henry's hard work at teaching George manners had paid off, with a few minor exceptions.

Henry nudged him. "George," he whispered. "You can slow down. I promise I'll let you eat your fill."

"Good advice for me as well," Bethan said.

"Yes, Sister. Come up for air," Elunid drawled, making George giggle.

"Would you mind passing me the chicken, George?" Elunid asked. "It's frightfully good, isn't it?"

George gulped before he said, "My favorite."

A companionable silence ensued as they tucked into their tea. She found herself glancing at Henry frequently. Did the food taste better because he shared it with her? He seemed different today, but she couldn't put her finger on it. More elegant, cultured, light-hearted?

Elunid glanced at Bethan. "You're staring at me."

"Oh, I'm sorry, *Chwaer*. It's just good to see you eating so well."

Elunid lifted one slender shoulder. "I'm hungry."

Bethan wiped a tear from her eye.

"What's the matter?"

"I'm happy for this day, Sister."

"I'm a burden to you."

"No." She grasped Elunid's hand. "You mustn't think it."

"I'm not often well."

"No," Bethan said.

"I'm sorry."

"It's not your fault."

Elunid's shoulders slumped. "You're wrong. It is most definitely my fault."

"Let's just enjoy this day, Elunid."

"Aye," Henry said. "It's a fine day indeed. And George…" He grinned. "What do you like to do best?"

"Eat."

"Besides eating."

"Sing."

"I know it's breaking my own rules of not singing at the table, but how about a song or two?"

"Oh, yes!"

"I'm sure our dinner companions wouldn't mind."

"Of course not," Bethan and Elunid chorused.

"Will you sing *with* us?" Henry asked.

Bethan shook her head. "No, I cannot."

"I know you can," Henry said.

Elunid poked her arm. "Would you make poor George unhappy on his special day?"

"Oh please, Mistress Bethan," George cried.

How could she say no to the boy?

****

And what could it harm? Besides, she was already singing on the inside.

"What shall we sing, George?"

His dark brows knit with concentration. "I don't know. I love so many songs."

Mistress Reynolds put glasses of sherry on the table. "How about 'My Thing is My Own?' "

"Why, madame! I can hardly believe a fine lady like yourself would allow us to sing such a bawdy song," Henry teased.

"I like the tune, and I've a good memory of it."

"Do you now?" He winked.

She slapped him lightly on the shoulder. "Oh, if I was only twenty years younger, I'd lead you on a merry chase, lad."

They laughed.

"I like the tune too," George said.

"Ah, from D'Urfey's *Wit and Mirth: Pills to Purge Melancholy*," Bethan said. "Bawdy, but fun. Shall we begin?"

The slightly shocked but captive audience roared at all the right places, and one couldn't help but notice how well Henry's voice and hers blended.

"A Master of Musick
Came with an intent,
To give me a lesson
On my instrument,

~*~

I thanked him for nothing,
But bid him be gone,
For my little fiddle,
Should not be played on."

They finished with a flourish, and the room erupted in applause. Elunid hadn't sung but held up her glass. "To George. May your thing be your own for many years to come."

"Oh, hear hear," Henry said.

Her sister had made a joke.

"I don't know what thing you mean, but I'll try," George said.

It felt so good to sing, as if part of her had been caged and had just been set free.

"I have a song," George said eagerly. "May I sing it, Da?"

"Yes, of course."

The room grew still.

> *"I love to live by the ocean.*
> *I love to live by the sea,*
> *When all the lovely mermaids,*
> *Swim up and sing to me.*

~*~

> *They tell me I am handsome,*
> *They tell me I am sweet,*
> *And they are very sorry,*
> *That they don't have feet."*

The room erupted in applause.

"Well done! Where did you hear it?"

"I made it up myself!"

"Goodness." Elunid grinned. "I like it very much."

George remained standing. "I am the king of birthdays, and this is my command: I would like my royal subjects"—he pointed at Bethan and Henry—"to sing a song together."

"A duet?" Henry glanced at Bethan. "Why not?"

She nodded.

"What shall we sing, George?"

"Hmm…how about 'I Thee Treasure'?"

"Stand up," George ordered.

Bethan cleared her throat and gripped the table's edge. All eyes in the room watched. This was maybe not such a good idea. She sat down.

"Bethan." His eyes held reassurance, his broad chest strength.

She rose, and at his nod, they began to sing. The room disappeared as she watched his mouth move, and the rise and fall of his chest. She let his rich bass consort with her soprano.

When they finished, the room was silent. Then the crowd cheered and waved their handkerchiefs in the air. Several women wiped their eyes.

Mistress Reynolds sniffed. "Took me back to my younger days. You make a fine pair, the two of you."

"She plays the pianoforte as well," Elunid said.

"Does she now?"

"Yes, she plays beautifully."

"Thank you, Sister."

Elunid shrugged. "'Tis true."

"This is fortuitous indeed," Henry said. "I helped Ian cart a pianoforte from the docks. Came in for him from France."

"You should have seen Maggie's face when we arrived with it. Apparently he'd not thought to mention it. She was none too pleased."

"We got out of there as fast as we could." George shuddered, making Elunid giggle.

She hadn't played in ever so long. Sometimes when Elunid had her bad days, Bethan retreated to her imagination, warm fingers on cool ivory. She reveled in the beauty of it, how the notes on the paper made perfect sense when so much of her life did not.

"We shall escort you over to see it," Henry said.

"Mayhap you'll play George a tune."

"Yes," Elunid said. "It's early yet. I've time yet before They call upon me."

Henry and Bethan exchanged glances. His eyes shone with perfect understanding and warm reassurance.

"Why not?" she said.

Chapter Twenty-Five

Why not indeed? Once outside, Henry offered Bethan his arm. How would it be to have her on his arm every day, feel her bright presence at his side to share life's duties? He hadn't thought he could want her more, but after hearing her sing...

He would request she wear the peacock dress when they married. The dress would overpower another woman, but on her it complemented her tall grace, made her eyes a darker blue.

He grasped her by the waist and spun her around. She squealed but smiled down at him. Yes, he would marry her.

He set her down again, and she backed away. "George is a wonderful boy."

He smiled. If they'd been alone, he would have kissed her then, put into it all the joy in his soul. "He's all a father could ask for." He took Bethan's hand, kissed it. "Thank you for making his birthday memorable."

Ian's harassed voice carried through their cottage window. "Woman, I insist you sit down and put your feet up."

"I'm fine. Do not order me about."

"Any fool can see you're exhausted, and there's no need to work yourself every damn minute of the day."

"I've never heard Ian sound so irate," Henry

whispered.

"I know my own body."

"Your feet were swollen last night, if you recall."

"It's very common."

"I don't like it. It's a sign you need to slow down, and you know it."

"You're being tiresome, Ian."

"I may be stuck in this chair, Maggie mine, but you *will* do as I say."

"He must be worried about her to be so cross. It isn't like him," Bethan said.

"We should stop eavesdropping," Henry said.

"Yes, I suppose it's wrong of us." She grinned mischievously.

His heart flopped in his chest like a landed lamprey. Henry opened the door for Bethan, and the room fell silent.

"Oh, hello!" Ian's nutmeg-colored hair stood on end.

Maggie stood, red-faced and panting.

****

Bethan took Maggie by the arm. "Let's go sit down." She guided her to the divan in the sitting room.

"What I've been trying to tell her," Ian muttered.

"We heard," Henry said drily.

Elunid and George stood at the threshold.

"I'll make some tea." Bethan motioned for them to come in.

Henry patted Ian on the back. "Ian, man! We've come to see your pianoforte."

"Ah, excellent! Let me finish something up here. It's a mixture for Captain Jacobs."

Maggie sank onto the divan. "Truthfully, I longed

to sit down, but he was being so dictatorial I had to argue."

Bethan snorted and lifted the midwife's feet to put the stool underneath them. "Your feet are *dreadfully* swollen. The ankles too."

Maggie nodded and closed her eyes. "I think I'll like this child better out than in."

Bethan almost dropped the teapot.

"You think it's funny now," Maggie said. "Wait until it's your turn."

"Me? No, it will never happen."

"Why?"

"My sister. She would be his burden as well."

Maggie opened her eyes, pierced her with her gray gaze. "Never underestimate the man you love. And you love him, do you not?"

"Well…"

"It's plain to see, Bethan."

Thankfully, Ian entered with Henry in tow. "The pianoforte is over in the corner."

"Yes, because we needed one more instrument." Maggie rubbed her forehead. "Though in truth I'm happy music soothes him somewhat."

"Is it your head again?" Ian wheeled over to Maggie, put his palm on her forehead.

"Yes, I've a headache," Maggie snapped. "Will you please stop fussing over me like an old crone?"

"I'll fix you something for it." He wheeled out of the room, quickly returning. He mixed the contents into her tea and gave it to her. "Take it. Now."

"Yes, yes. Go show them your new toy."

Ian shook his head, then led the way. "It's over here in the corner."

"Oh, do you mind?" Bethan excused herself and joined them.

"Of course not," Maggie said. "I'll close my eyes for a bit."

It was a thing of great beauty, carved wooden and glowing.

"I just finished polishing it," Ian said.

"Oh. It's exquisite, so much finer than the one I played."

"You play?"

"Yes, though it's been a long time."

"Wonderful!" He clapped his hands. "You can teach me."

"But Mr. Ian," George cried. "You play all manner of instruments."

"To be honest, the piano is not my forte." He waggled his eyebrows.

Maggie groaned.

"Sit down, Bethan." Ian ordered.

Henry pulled the bench out for her. "Please, dear."

Ian shot him a glance. "Ah?"

"Play something, Sister," Elunid said.

"Well, I…" The keys beckoned to her.

"Please, Miss Bethan," George said.

Elunid retreated to the divan with Maggie.

Bethan turned around. "Elunid, will you fetch Maggie her tea?" Yes, she was steady enough to do it.

Ian handed her some sheet music. "Here, can you play this?"

One of her favorites. Thomas Tallis composed for Henry VIII, Queen Elizabeth, and Queen Mary as well. "I haven't played in ever so long. I'll be rusty." Her heart raced as she scanned the music. What if she didn't remember? A broad hand squeezed her shoulder lightly and rested there.

She took a deep breath. The keys were cool against her heated fingers. She began to play the opening notes, tentative and soft at first, but soon the room around her dissolved, and her heart opened like a new rose.

"This has lyrics."

Henry's deep voice jolted her out of her reverie, and she struck a bad note.

"I'm sorry. I didn't mean to distract you," he said.

"Just so, just so," Ian murmured, an amused lilt to his voice.

"Yes, Henry." She'd said his given name without thinking, and on her lips it felt as intimate as a kiss. "But they're in Latin."

He nodded. "Carry on, Mistress Bethan."

She played the opening lines, and his bass voice banished all rational thought and surrounded her senses, as her fingers on the keys joined him in a dance.

He knew Latin. How could a man with such humble origins speak Latin so flawlessly? Her fingers trembled on the keys. He leaned forward to turn the page, warmth radiating from his chest. His breath caressed her neck, making her tingle all the way to her breasts. Every inch of her body felt alive and warm.

As Henry turned the final page, the music ended. She couldn't contain a disappointed sigh.

"You play beautifully," Henry said.

She held her fingers in front of her, feeling as if they belonged to someone else. "I could scarcely believe I remembered how to play."

"Your fingers remembered."

"Yes."

His eyes had turned black as the minor keys, and as full of possibilities. He fingered the sheet music. "Do you know what this song is about?"

"I don't read Latin."

The bench was big enough for the both of them; she motioned for him to sit. The side of his hard thighs burned through her dress, and she had a momentary flash of memory like lightning in darkness, of feeling his bare thighs against her light summer dress.

He cleared his throat. "Bethan?"

"Yes?"

"You had the most peculiar expression on your face."

Pray God he didn't know what she was thinking.

"I asked how you came to be interested in the music of Thomas Tallis." He rested his strong muscular fingers on the keys.

"Years ago, a friend of my father came to visit. He was a skilled pianist, and he carried his music with him wherever he went. He left this very piece for me." She stopped, opened her mouth to speak, promptly closed it.

"What is it?" His voice was very gentle.

"It's just that…I'd forgotten. When I play the piano and the music sinks into me, I'm not my sister's keeper. I am just myself. I can forget my life, escape into my own world, instead of always being in hers."

"Yes." He was so close she could hear his heart beat. "It's how I feel when we're together."

Joy rushed through her like a spring fed river. She nodded, gratified at the look of warm pleasure in his eyes. "You do not think us selfish?"

"I feel no shame about my feelings for you, Bethan."

"It's impossible."

"How can I convince you it's not?"

She couldn't look at him. "I would be both selfish and foolish to expect anyone to carry my burden."

"Have faith in me, Bethan. I would do anything for you."

"You're only human."

"Can you not see we're meant to be together?"

She cleared her throat and put the pages in order. "If I play it again, can you sing it in English?"

"I'll try. Bethan, you can change the subject all you want, but we *will* be together."

She tried to remain unaffected by what he said, but anger warmed her face. He didn't know what life required of her. How could she give herself to him when she could not give herself fully?

Then, the notes on the page, so precise and predictable, soothed her as they always had. The music and his deep voice singing of praise and faith were over too soon.

"Thank you. I like the words, but I think it sounds better in Latin."

"I wish I could kiss you, Bethan. Slowly, thoroughly, and privately."

She nodded. Just because it was impossible didn't mean she didn't want it.

"Sister, I need thread."

She released his hand, and he groaned.

She rose. "Elunid, I need to speak with Maggie for a few minutes, and then I'll take you."

"Time is running out," her twin said.

"I lost track of time."

"Clearly." She looked anxiously toward the door.

"George could take her," Henry said.

"Yes," said George. "I'm tired of sitting."

Henry reached into his pocket. "If I know you, you're probably hungry again. Fetch yourself and Elunid something at the bakers."

"Thank you, Da!"

She studied Elunid; there was nothing in her manner to hint of oncoming trouble. "Why not?"

"How nice of you to give me permission." Elunid rolled her eyes.

"Take my arm, Elunid," George said.

To Bethan's surprise, she linked her arm with his.

"I'll meet you at the notions shop in a bit."

Ian and Maggie were drinking tea on the divan.

"It's time, Maggie," Ian said. "Tell her."

"Tell me what?"

Maggie sighed. "I know he's right. Bethan. I feel it won't be long until the baby comes."

As if in answer, her stomach shifted, and an odd look passed over her face.

Henry fetched the teapot and filled their cups.

He stood in front of Ian, who tapped the fingers of his free hand on his lap, beating out a complicated rhythm.

"Hold still, man," Henry said.

Ian held out his cup. "Sorry."

Maggie sighed. "I know you're trying to keep me company, and your effort is appreciated, but you're vexing me."

His brows rose. He hoisted himself up, holding onto the edge of the divan, and reached for the handles of the wheelchair. "Clever of you to put locks on this chair, Henry." He settled in his wheeling chair and grinned. "Once again, I thank you, my friend." He promptly made his way over to the pianoforte.

"Bethan, are you ready to become the town's midwife?"

"Yes, of course." She hoped she sounded more confident than she felt.

"You have already delivered one child, with minimal help from me."

"Yes." But she would have to do it all alone, and the first babe she delivered would likely be Maggie's.

Why did she torture herself with dreams of a normal life? Just because Elunid had a good day, didn't mean she would have one tomorrow. Her shoulders slumped under the weight of worry.

Maggie had misinterpreted her, no doubt. "Don't worry, Bethan. You'll do fine."

"If your midwifery skills are equal to your piano playing skills, you're a force to be reckoned with indeed!" Ian said.

"Agreed."

"What would you men know about it?" Bethan asked.

"It's heartening to see your sister doing so well. Was it my medicine, do you suppose?" A look of childlike hope lit Ian's eyes.

Bethan shrugged. "I'm not sure. It helped calm her to a certain extent last night, but she didn't receive any this morning, and she's been better than I've seen her in ages."

"I'll keep working on it, and no time like the present." Ian glanced at Maggie. "My reasons are a tad selfish; a remedy that helps her may help me as well. I must be my best self for the babe and my Maggie." He wheeled behind the divan, kissed the top of Maggie's head. "Come, Henry. We've not talked in a while, and I'll slip you some medicine before you leave, Bethan."

Maggie rose, and Bethan rushed to assist her. She waddled over to the bookcase, grabbed her midwife basket, and handed it to Bethan.

"Here you go. You'll find everything you need in it. I just replenished the supplies this morning."

When Bethan reached to take it, Maggie tugged back, slightly.

Maggie sighed and released her hold. "It was my life and reason for living before I met Ian. You can't blame me for wanting to hold onto it."

"Of course not," Bethan said, responsibility weighing on her. "I have impossible shoes to fill." She glanced down at Maggie's feet. "Even if they are swollen."

"Ha ha," Maggie said. "I've faith in you, Bethan. Don't forget, I expect you to come and fill me in on what's happening with our ladies, and even if I'm big as a boat, I can still give advice."

Bethan hugged her, held her at arm's length. "You're quite beautiful, Maggie."

"Away with you," Maggie said.

"Yes. I need to retrieve Elunid and get her—and this basket—home."

"I believe I'll lie down a bit."

Bethan helped Maggie onto the divan and tucked a blanket on her legs.

"Thank you, Bethan."

Henry and Ian stood behind the counter, heads together.

"I'm going to fetch Elunid now," Bethan said.

"Goodbye, Ian."

Before she could blink an eye, Henry appeared at her side. "I'll carry your basket for you."

"No," Bethan said. "I must, for it makes my new vocation seem more real."

He nodded. "I understand. May I take your arm?"

He might as well, for he already had her heart.

As if in punishment her for her selfish turn of phrase, they happened upon Elunid and Isadora on the docks, heads together. George stood, wringing his hands, eyes following a retreating figure. Charlotte.

"Something's amiss," Bethan murmured.

When they approached, Isadora slunk away, a secretive smile on her pockmarked face. Bethan felt the absence of warmth as she broke away from Henry.

Henry put his hand on George's shoulder. "What's the matter, son?"

"I don't know, but look at Elunid. The light's gone out of her. I wanted to come get you, but I didn't want to leave her."

Elunid's fingers clenched in her skirts, marring the beautiful fabric, lips moving in a soundless conversation.

"Ellie."

She flinched at Bethan's touch.

"What did they say to you?"

No answer. Henry and George joined them.

"George, do you know what they said to her?" she asked.

"No, I couldn't understand. I'm so stupid, and now her light's gone out."

"George, it's not your fault," Henry said.

"Sister, did they make sport of you?"

Finally Elunid shook her head but kept her eyes lowered.

"They said something about tomorrow, how it would happen tomorrow," George said. "And when I asked them what they meant, they said I was too stupid to understand."

"No, George."

"Look, you've dirtied your dress, Elunid." Bethan said. "Let's go home and change out of our finery."

See, Henry? This is why I cannot have a life of my own.

As they walked to the Siren Inn, Henry had his arm around George's shoulder, and Bethan had one arm around Elunid's, the basket in the other one. All she could do was tend to Elunid's physical needs, the only thing she could control.

****

By the time they arrived at the Siren Inn, the mood had turned sober, and his heart ached to see the slump of resignation in Bethan's shoulders.

When Lena took Elunid by the hand, Henry grasped Bethan's. "I wish I could take this burden from you."

"It's my burden to bear." Without another word, she turned and joined her sister.

A fair number of customers already filled the tables, as early as it was.

"Ah, *du bist shon*!"

"What did she say, Da?"

"I said you look handsome, George!" Lena ruffled his hair.

"Lena," Bethan said. "I'm sorry we tarried so long."

"No, beautiful *fräulein*. Everyone deserves a little holiday."

"I'll change my clothes and join you."

"George, take off your topcoat and hang it up. Take mine as well," Henry ordered.

George approached Elunid, whose eyes darted around the room. When George took her hand, she smiled.

"Thank you for your company, Miss Elunid." He bowed.

His gallant lad.

Elunid bowed her head gracefully, then grew stiff again.

"Come, Elunid. Let's get our work-a-day clothes on."

When they married, they would lift each other up, comfort each other through life's ever-changing currents.

He watched her retreating form until she disappeared, feeling Bethan's pain as his own. The snuffing out of Elunid's bright spark was like a death to her.

At least he could ease her workload. "George, would you like to clear tables tonight? Can you be careful enough?"

"Of course, Da! I'm almost a man now."

He stifled a laugh and put on his apron. Mayhap he could comfort Bethan later tonight.

Chapter Twenty-Six

"I have frittered away the day. They'll not be happy about that," Elunid muttered.

Bethan helped her out of her dress and into some everyday attire. "You've plenty of time, Elunid." No sense in trying to talk Elunid out of her thoughts. "Did we not have a wonderful time?"

She hung up Elunid's dress, while Elunid bent to retrieve her sewing basket on the floor. "Did we not confound the town with our foolery?"

"Just like when we were girls." But the lilt was gone from Elunid's voice. "Young George is a good lad."

"You have an affinity, the two of you."

"Inasmuch as anyone could." Elunid sat in the chair by the bed, reaching in her basket for the cloth. "I've made progress, but it's not enough." She bent to her work.

Bethan swallowed her impatience and tried to gauge Elunid's state of mind: lucid, but single-minded. Good. She had better get to work.

"I'll be checking on you later."

"No need. *They'll* be checking on me."

If only she could see into her mind. Maybe then she could understand her better. She shut the door quietly and headed for the taproom. At the entrance, she took a deep breath and pasted a smile on her face.

Henry smiled at her, his eyes upon her in blessing, and she pulled her shoulders up and smiled in reply.

She barely had time to think of her sister's odd behavior during the busy evening. And every time she passed Henry, he touched her in some way, if not with the gentle reassurance of his fingers upon her arm, then with a warm glance. In spite of her burden, she seemed to float on air, like a gull lifting with the breeze. She relaxed and enjoyed the excitement of the evening, for she and Elunid were the talk of the town.

"How do we know you're not Elunid?" Ed the butcher said.

"Oh, trust me. You'd never catch her waiting on the likes of you." She laughed.

"Fetch me some more of that summer ale, Miss Bethan."

Henry appeared with a large tray of food. She rushed to help him distribute the fragrant comestibles, as Maggie and Ian came through the door.

She straightened. "Maggie, why are you not at home with your feet up?"

"Oh, please don't chastise me, Bethan. I've heard it enough already."

Ian ran his long fingers through his hair, which already stood on end. "She is impossible and stubborn beyond belief!"

The babe looked as if it had dropped some more, and Maggie could barely walk. Even her face seemed swollen.

"She's allowed out long enough to have some of your fried haddock, for which she has a powerful craving," Ian said.

Henry rushed to place a chair under the midwife

and took another one nearby to put her feet upon.

"I wish you'd all stop fussing with me. I'm not helpless."

Bethan leaned to whisper in Maggie's ear. "I've been reading in the midwife book. It says your headache is caused by ill vapors. There's naught to be done about it, as you know, but to give you some cinnamon water mixed with white wine, by the spoonful. Are you already doing it?"

Maggie's brows rose. "Very good, Bethan. I have been taking it, and it's not helping."

"Right, then." Bethan patted her on the shoulder. "It won't be long, Maggie. Take heart."

Ian handed Maggie a mug of ale, kissed her forehead.

A fanciful thought flitted through Bethan's mind unbidden. What would it be like, to carry Henry's child? Would he be as solicitous, tender? *Stop it, Bethan. Stop wishing for things you can't have.* And suddenly she wanted very much to carry his sweetness inside of her.

Henry gazed at her, as if he'd read her thoughts. "Is all well, Bethan?"

"Henry, give Mistress Maggie my fish. I'll wait for some more," Ed the butcher said.

Maggie nodded her thanks. "As many babes as I've brought into the world, I had no idea how the little beasts can take over a body."

The drummer of the Wandering Wastrels marched through the open door, beating his drum, and soon the inn was engaged in a rousing sing-along, with Charlotte and Reggie in fine fettle indeed.

Reggie approached her. "Where is my peacock?"

"The peacock's in the closet, where she belongs."

"I'm sorry to hear it, my queen. I…"

Henry appeared and put his hand upon her arm possessively.

Reggie's eyes took note, and he nodded, as if to himself. "I'm thirsty. Fetch me something, Henry."

Henry let out a burst of air, and Charlotte swept up beside him with a rustle of silk skirts. Bethan couldn't help but stare at her bosom, which reminded her of two rolls left to rise too long. The vixen batted her eyelashes at Henry.

Henry smiled.

"You seem different, Henry." She advanced, pressed her bodice against him.

Did he fancy her? She was very fetching, with a delicate face and pouty full lips, not to mention the generous figure she seemed to want to share with everyone.

"Same old night soil man," he said, backing away.

She made a face. "For a moment there, I forgot who you really were."

He seemed not the least bit bothered by her comment but turned and winked at Bethan.

"Come, Charlotte. Let's sing, since my ale is not forthcoming." Reggie gave Henry the gimlet eye.

"More music, you lazy dolts!" Widow Jenkins slammed her mug on the table.

The Wandering Wastrels picked up their instruments and filled the room with bawdy tunes. Ian's imprisonment in a wheelchair in no way inhibited him from participating, and Bethan caught the glowing admiration on Maggie's face as he belted out a tune. George joined him with a natural harmony, making the crowd roar with admiration.

When she entered the kitchen, Henry put his hands on her waist and wheeled her around. "What a day it's been, hasn't it, Bethan?"

The way he said her name, his low voice resonating deep within her belly. No one had picked her up since her father. Henry made her feel as light and delicate as one of Mrs. Reynold's teacakes. He set her down slowly, making her body brush against him. She couldn't think, could only imagine what it would feel like to be pressed together, skin to skin.

"I would like to talk with you later, Bethan." The intimate tone in his voice made her watch his lips.

"Yes, after I clean up."

"After *we* clean up. I'm at your side, Bethan. It's where I belong." He rested his palms on her temples and kissed her on the forehead, his lips lingering for a moment, but not long enough.

She stared after him as he walked into the crowded room. Was she a fool to believe he would stay by her side? If he did, he'd be the first one who did. As she followed him out, she caught Widow Jenkin's sly wink, as if she knew her blush came from more than a hot kitchen.

Later in the evening, Isadora and Charlotte sat in the corner by the fireplace with their heads together. Why would Charlotte bother with the provincial Isadora?

She reached their table. "Would you like something to drink?"

Charlotte made a big show of peering up at her, to make sport of her height. "Perhaps a glass of wine? Or mayhap I should just ask for vinegar. For it will surely taste the same."

Isadora tittered. "I'll have one too."

Silly girl. She knew Isadora preferred ale. She couldn't help a twinge of sympathy for her; she wanted so badly to belong. Her father was immersed in a game of chance, paying no heed to her.

"Most people drink ale, because of Lena's skill," Bethan said.

"Of course they do," Charlotte said." I don't know why Reggie insists on staying here so long."

Bethan shook her head and made her way back to the counter. She unearthed an old bottle of claret and poured two glasses.

On her way back, she stopped by Maggie and Ian's table. "Can I fetch you anything else?"

Maggie burped and patted her belly. "I can't have another bite, though this little beast is begging me to."

"I told you we would not stay long." Ian wheeled around to her side of the table and placed her cloak about her shoulders.

She rolled her eyes. "Yes, I know." She turned to Bethan. "I'm not used to being idle."

Bethan grinned. "You'll be busy soon enough, Maggie. Enjoy the rest."

Ian's eyes were intent upon her as she slowly stood. "Hold onto my handles for support."

Maggie nodded, and they made their slow way out the door.

Isadora's father fetched her from the table, gaping at Charlotte for a moment. As they exited, he said, "Why were you talking to that baggage? If your mother gets wind of this, she'll likely slap you silly."

Isadora cringed.

The inn began thinning out, and soon even the Wandering Wastrels trailed away.

Bethan sent Sabine and Lena to bed, and soon only she and Henry remained. They tidied up in companionable silence.

Bethan wiped the sweat from her forehead with a corner of her apron. "Thank you for your help."

He nodded and glanced at George, who lay stretched out in front of the fire. "Poor lad. We'll have to get to work soon. It's almost morning. It was a grand day, wasn't it? Just the birthday he wanted." He turned to her. "Thank you for making it special for him."

"He's a fine boy. Elunid and I enjoyed the day as well."

He grasped her hands. "Come outside for a moment, Bethan." The sound of her name from his lips, so intimate, made her center glow like a hot coal. She nodded.

They stood in the little courtyard, hands clasped, listening to the sounds of people headed home from their revelries, the clanging of a ship's bell echoing from the water.

He cleared his voice. "Bethan."

She nodded.

"I'd very much like to kiss you."

She leaned toward him. He took off her cap, smoothed her hair down with a touch so gentle it brought tears to her eyes.

"So soft," he whispered. He traced the contours of her face with his fingertips and kissed her, a slow, searching kiss, making her center pulse. His lips were soft and full.

She kissed him back, felt the curve of his smile

against her lips. She put her arms around him, pulled him closer to stroke his muscular broad back.

Hold me tighter, Henry. She opened her mouth to better taste him, lay her tongue against his, exploring the rough texture and wet warmth of it.

He wrapped his arms around her, held her against his arousal. His hands cupped her buttocks; she rocked against the hard length of him and gasped.

He broke away. "We should stop, before…and George and I must make our rounds."

She nodded and put herself to rights, avoiding his eyes. "And I must check on Elunid."

"Look at me, sweeting."

She met his dark gaze and he kissed her again. "I would begin and end every day with your kiss."

He took her arm, and they returned to their responsibilities. How could it be otherwise?

Chapter Twenty-Seven

"I'm so tired, Da."

"One step at a time, George. When we play, we must pay."

"My legs ache."

"What would happen if the cesspits overflowed because we didn't feel like emptying them? How would we have the coin for food if we didn't do our job?"

"All right."

"Heave ho. We'll be done before you know it. How about a song? 'Twill make the time go faster."

"Look at the moon."

"It will be full tomorrow. Do we know a song about the moon?"

He'd like to write a song about the moonlight on Bethan's face. She'd be alarmed if she knew how close he'd come to giving in to his animal urges, to take her there in the moonlight, raising her skirts, running his hands up the long length of her white thighs…

"Da, what should we sing?"

"How about 'My Golden Moon'?"

Bethan in his arms and in his bed would be a reality, but he would marry her first. Could he give her more in his other life? Not without sacrificing George.

****

Bethan checked on Elunid, who could not be persuaded to go to bed. She walked into her own room, undressed, and climbed into bed, limbs thrumming with fatigue, yet she couldn't settle. If she ran her tongue on her lips she could still taste him. If she closed her eyes, she could feel his arms strong and banded about her body, the hard bulge of his manhood against her thighs. She wanted…she didn't know exactly what she wanted.

Her mind drifted. They were alone with only the moon for company. He stood by the water's edge, removed his linen shirt, his eyes intent upon her all the while. He'd taken off his shirt with a slight smile on his face. She took in his powerful shoulders, the banded strength of his chest, curly dark hair covering his chest and tapering to a place beyond his waistband.

With his eyes still on her, he removed his breeches, and stood, tall, proud. He beckoned to her, and she followed without question. His eyes wandered down her bodice, he lifted his brows in question, waited until she nodded, then slowly unlaced it, letting it drop to the floor. He untied the string to her shift, and it slipped off her like a spirit leaving a body. He led her into the water, the waist-deep warmth rippling upon her naked body, the chill of the night air making her nipples harden.

He pulled her against him so she could feel the rough texture of his hair, the hard planes of muscle, smooth, hard manhood between her legs.

"Bethan!"

Elunid stood at the head of her bed, hair tousled, eyes wide. "They are merciful. The sun is up." She peered at her. "You're all red. Are you feverish?"

Yes, but not with sickness. "I'm fine." How long had it been since her twin had shown concern for her?

"They are wrong."

"Who?" She grabbed her robe and splashed her face with cool water from the basin.

Elunid stamped her foot. "The plumed lady."

"What?"

"Plumed." She gestured about her head. "Tiny. Sharp voice. Blonde."

"Charlotte?"

"Yes, Charlotte the harlot. And the pockmarked chit."

"Isadora."

"Yes, who cares?"

"Why don't you tell me what this is all about."

Elunid opened the curtains, her pale face radiant. "Look, the sun has risen. The pockmarked chit and harlot said this morning would be the day the sun would not rise, and it would be my fault, as I'd suspected. But they were wrong. They were wrong, Bethan."

"Of course they were wrong, Elunid. They were just trying to confuse you, encourage your…ideas."

"I've been given an extra day."

"No, Elunid. They were only trying to upset you. Isadora had overheard you the other day, and the two women wanted to upset you, that's all."

What could they hope to accomplish? She needed to talk to Henry about this, ask his advice.

And then, as if the conversation had never happened, Elunid rushed from the room. "I must get to work. I may only have the day, before darkness falls evermore."

Elunid would need watching over today. She knew the signs well enough by now.

She fixed her tea and opened the door to the inn. She couldn't begin to fathom the troubled sea of her sister's mind. Better she recall her dream, feel his lips upon hers again. Why shouldn't she snatch whatever happiness she could? She'd be a damn fool to deny the urgings of her body, the way he made her feel treasured and protected. And alive.

She opened the inn door and stood sipping her tea. Like any other morning, the creak of the wagon and the soft singing voices of Henry and George carried up the street, as much a part of the dawn as birdsong.

Henry approached, standing at a distance.

"Come closer," she said.

"Oh."

He stood a few feet in front of her. How strange—whatever revulsion she had about his job had disappeared like fog in sunlight.

He grinned. "I've a question to ask you, Bethan."

She nodded.

"Would you accompany me on a moonlight picnic tonight? The moon is full, like last night." He glanced at her lips.

She forced herself to inhale. "Yes, yes, of course." So eager. He must think her the biggest fool. And moonlight? She blushed, thinking of her dream.

"Excellent. I will have a picnic made: cheese, wine, bread."

"I've never had a picnic under the moon."

"Neither have I," he said. "It will be a memorable night for thee and me."

She must snatch happiness where she could.

"I must go, but I'll see you tonight."

She wished he would kiss her, occupation be damned.

Chapter Twenty-Eight

The morning flew by, and Bethan kept one eye open for the appearance of Isadora or Charlotte, and an eye out for Elunid, who'd been sewing all day without ceasing.

"Elunid. Stop for a while. Come and have a bite to eat."

"I dare not." Her face was white as whey, and her fingers trembled as she held the cloth. Thank God Ian had given her more medicine. She would wait and see if her condition worsened.

She went about her duties, spent some time in Elunid's room, studying the midwife book Maggie had loaned her. So many puzzling and unsettling instructions. How would she ever know what to do?

Later that afternoon, she watched Lena make beer when Ian's messenger boy came to tell her Maggie was in labor.

"Go, *Liebchen*. Sabine and I will watch over your sister."

"Come quickly," the boy said.

Trepidation filled Bethan as she made her way over to the cottage, midwife basket in hand. She knew so little, she'd wager she didn't even know all the things that could go wrong. Ignorance. She should have studied more. No, this would not do. She must have faith. She must pray. She'd already delivered two babes; she would deliver Maggie's safely. She lifted her shoulders and soon arrived at the cottage.

"Thank God you're here," Ian whispered. "She has a fierce headache, and nothing I give her will relieve it."

Was such a severe headache normal?

He tried to make light of it in his usual fashion. "She wants to kill something. Me. I deserve it, for I got her in this condition. The headache could just be the goldenrod blooming, which she said has often bedeviled her in the past. I don't know."

With more confidence than she felt, Bethan put a hand on his shoulder. "She'll be fine, Ian."

"Ack!"

Bethan rushed into the parlor.

"Yes, Maggie. How can I help you?"

Maggie stood in the middle of the parlor, one palm holding her forehead, one hand holding up her skirts. "You can fetch me some towels. My waters just broke."

"Holy hell!" Ian grabbed a stack of linen on the divan and handed one to Maggie.

"Time to get your dress off. Let's make you comfortable."

"That's what he said nine months ago, and look at me now."

"I didn't hear you complain about it then, my love."

Bethan burst out laughing, and her nervousness disappeared. She could do this. As she helped Maggie out of her dress, Maggie bent with a pain. "Oh, they really are stronger once the waters break! You see, nature has planned it so, Bethan."

"Stop instructing. You're the patient," Ian said.

"He's right. Now, lie down in front of the fire, and I'll take off your stockings." Bethan shook her head at the grossly swollen ankles and feet. She exchanged a worried glance with Ian.

"It's the strangest sensation, breaking your waters," Maggie murmured.

"I got the pallet prepared just in time," Ian exclaimed.

"Oh, my head," Maggie moaned.

"I'm sorry. I can't give you anything else, Maggie. I'll fetch a cold cloth."

"How far apart are the pains?" Bethan asked.

"About three minutes."

"I must put a closed sign on the door," Ian said.

"Yes, I don't need an audience."

A few minutes later, Maggie cast a glance at Ian, who was still in the shoppe room.

"Something is wrong, Bethan," she whispered.

"I'm sure every mother thinks so at this point."

"No, you must call on the Holy Nun. She will help us." She grasped Bethan's hand.

"Promise me."

"I will, Maggie." If it helped her friend to hear it.

"Believe in her, Bethan."

She felt like a hypocrite, for how could she believe in this Holy Nun, when she wasn't even sure about God's mercy? But nevertheless, she bowed her head. "Be with us, Holy Mother, as we bring another child in the world. Keep Maggie and the babe safe."

Maggie nodded, the wrinkled furrows in her forehead lessening a bit.

"Thank you, Bethan."

She nodded. "Are you ready to bring your child

into the world?"

Maggie grunted. "I want it to be over."

She'd gone very pale all of a sudden. "My head, it hurts so. God help me."

"It's a little soon, but I'll give you a dose of willow bark." Ian wheeled into the shoppe.

Bethan reached into her basket and brought out a flask of white wine boiled with mugwort. She had learned it would fortify Maggie and hopefully ease the delivery.

She handed the flask to Ian. "Give her a teaspoonful every so often."

A vein beat in Maggie's forehead, fast and out of measure. Unease prickled down Bethan's spine. The sooner she delivered the child, the better.

Please, dear Holy Nun, if you're with us, help her.

"I'll check you now, and we will see how your sweet babe is doing."

Maggie nodded.

Bethan put oil of almonds on her hands and examined the passage, "Maggie, you're progressing well. This is much faster than little Emma's delivery. You don't have far to go until your passage is fully open for the babe."

"Anything could happen, Bethan."

"Take heart, my Maggie." Ian had gotten out of his wheelchair and sat by Maggie's head, leaning against the wooden makeshift bed for support.

She didn't know much, but she knew men didn't stay for the delivery. "Ian, why don't you go over to the Siren Inn to wait?"

"No. I won't leave her."

"But Ian," Maggie pleaded. "It's not done."

There was no mistaking the steel in his voice. "I will be right here with you, Maggie. I will see my child safely into this world, and see you through your travail."

She could tell there would be no persuading him.

Well then. She would put him to work. "Does your back ache, Maggie?"

"What do you think?" she snapped.

Without Bethan having to instruct him, Ian rubbed Maggie's lower back.

Another contraction hit Maggie.

"Breathe, sweeting. It will abate soon. It's a good, strong one." Bethan tried to keep her voice calm, but her heart beat so loud she could barely think.

"My sweet warrior," Ian murmured, his voice knife-edged with rust. "You are brave beyond measure."

The pain abated.

"Has your headache lessened at all, Maggie?"

She didn't answer Bethan. At this time in her travails, a woman goes inside herself to seek communion with her child, to both give and receive the strength to endure.

An hour passed, and the intensity and strength of the labor pains increased. Ian fed her the white wine with mugwort between pains. When the pains abated, Maggie sank back onto the pillow and all but fainted.

Bethan checked her progress. "It is almost time for you to push. A few more pains, and you'll be ready. You've been very brave. I think I would scream loud enough to raise the roof."

"Give me time," Maggie whispered.

The two women laughed, and Ian winced.

A new onslaught of pain came, and Maggie sought Bethan's gaze, eyes imploring her to take the pain away. Bethan wanted to look away from such suffering, but she could not, for it was her duty to bear witness.

"Lie on your side, Maggie. I'll massage your back."

Bethan helped Maggie roll over, and Ian used his thumbs to apply pressure on her lower back.

"Ah."

Another pain came on, and Maggie slapped his hands away, then reached for them.

"Right, love. Squeeze my hands."

"Breathe, Maggie. Don't hold your breath. This pain will not last forever, and you will soon have the babe in your arms."

Bethan wiped the sweat from her friend's face with a cold cloth soaked in lavender. Her unease began to lessen. Maggie was doing fine, and it seemed to help having Ian there. He leaned close and murmured words of comfort in her ear.

After the next pain, Bethan checked her progress. She was ready to push.

"Your passage is open. You can push with the next contraction. Close your eyes and ready yourself."

No sooner had Maggie closed her eyes than another pain barreled into her. Ian got behind her to help her sit.

"You must take a deep breath and push this time. Push with all your might."

A few more pushes.

"I see the head, Maggie."

"I cannot do this," she moaned.

"You can, my brave warrior," Ian crooned. "You

will be holding our babe in your arms soon."

There was scarcely time for Maggie to catch her breath before the assault of another contraction.

Bethan's hands shook with excitement and fear. "The head is emerging, Maggie. Nutmeg-colored hair like Ian's. Take a deep breath, and hold it now. Push."

My God, she didn't even scream.

"The head is out. Well done." She cradled the slick head, covered with a white substance.

Another pain came. It would be the shoulders next. *Turn them, Bethan.*

"Oh God, Ian!" Maggie had hold of his hands.

"I see the head, Maggie. A fine head! It will be over soon."

Then, with a huge, ragged breath, and a strangled cry, Maggie bore down.

Bethan braced the slick little head and turned the shoulders to ease their way out. One more push and the rest of the body slid out so quickly she had to rush to hold it.

"Ah," Maggie cried.

"It's a boy."

The baby cried, a low, husky keening. Bethan wiped the white matter off his face and wrapped him in a blanket.

Ian reached over and grasped the bundle. "Oh, my sweet boy. Oh God." He placed it into Maggie's arms, while Bethan tied off the cord, waiting to cut it until it stopped pulsing.

"He is beautiful. My boy." Maggie crooned.

Ian encircled his arms around her and the child. "My love. Thank you." The tension washed from Bethan's body at the scene.

"More pains as the afterburden comes out," Bethan said.

When the afterburden emerged, Bethan placed it in a basin and examined it carefully. It was intact. She fetched a basin and readied to clean Maggie up, relief washing the tension from her body.

"No." Ian took the basin and cloth from her. "Let me." As he saw the bloody results of childbirth, his face went slack. "Oh God. What she has done for me."

Maggie put the baby to breast. "My sweeting. You're finally here."

Ian set to work cleaning her with the utmost tenderness.

Suddenly, Maggie closed her eyes, her face contorted. "Oh, sweet Jesus. My head."

"I'll fetch you something." Ian broke away.

Then Maggie's head fell back on the pillow and she convulsed, great tremors quaking her body.

Ian dropped the basin. "Maggie!"

Bethan rescued the babe from her arms and placed him in the cradle.

Maggie had turned the color of a gravestone, and her pulse beat at an unholy rate. She convulsed again, back arching.

Bethan held her arms down. "No, Maggie."

As quickly as it had come on, the spasms left her body and she struggled for breath. "The baby?"

"The baby is fine, Maggie," Ian said.

Another convulsion took hold.

"Maggie!" Ian struggled to hold her.

With everything she possessed, Bethan cried, "Holy Mother, please save this woman, this giver of life. Please. Save her."

But another great tremor ripped through Maggie, and her eyes rolled back into her head.

"Please, Holy Mother," Bethan pleaded.

"Maggie!"

They would lose her. They could do nothing to help her.

Without warning, a woman's voice resounded inside Bethan's body. "Lay your hands on her, midwife."

Maggie shook with another onslaught, her face gray, spittle flying.

"Maggie," Ian shouted.

Bethan's hands filled with a life not her own. They hummed and pulsed with heat.

"Lay your hands on her, midwife," the voice said.

As Maggie convulsed, Bethan put her hands on her, a shock of power making her recoil. She touched her again, from head to shoulders, breasts to belly, each part stilling as she did so.

As she reached the bloody source of life, the birth passage, the shaking of Maggie's legs stopped. Maggie grew still, her breathing steady and sure.

Ian smoothed the hair from her face, putting his cheek against Maggie's. "My love. Rest now."

The warm power still coursed through Bethan's body. "Holy Mother be praised," she cried, and sank to her knees.

"What happened?' Maggie lifted her head.

Tears flowed down Bethan's face as a spirit of goodness and light enveloped her.

Ian held a cup of water to Maggie's lips. "You had convulsions."

Bethan rose and grasped Maggie's hands. "The

Holy Nun put her hands upon me and told me what to do. It was a miracle."

Maggie nodded. "I feel inordinately tired, but well. I feel her presence even now."

Tears rolled down her face, and Ian reached over and wiped them with one long finger.

"Why? Why would She choose me to save when so many die?"

"We will never know. But I am glad of it!"

"I want my babe," Maggie said.

Ian cleared his throat. "I'll fetch him." He struggled to stand and lifted their son from the cradle.

"He must nurse," Maggie said.

The babe latched on, and Maggie rested her lips upon his downy head. She was pale, but radiant. "You did well, Bethan."

"As did you."

Bethan put more water in the basin and set to work washing Maggie's privities.

"Here, let me." Ian made to join her.

"Stay with me, Ian."

He embraced her, hard enough to make the babe snuffle with irritation at getting ousted off his mother's nipple. "Of course."

"Yes, I'll take care of this straightaway," Bethan said.

In time, she had Maggie cleaned up, a new night rail on, and had given them a fortifying mug of ale. Her work done for the moment, she slumped down on the divan and tried to slow her racing heart. All was well. Maggie was weak but had no headache. The babe brimmed with good health and had a lusty cry. She exhaled a shaky breath and took a sip of her ale.

Her heart swelled with equal measures of pride and humility, and she gazed upon the couple. She had helped Ian sit behind Maggie so she could lean against him, and their arms encircled the babe, his little face red with squalling. The Holy Nun's hands still lay upon her in blessing, and her body hummed still with Her power.

Chapter Twenty-Nine

After she finished her ale, Bethan rose, joints creaking. She would go into the shop area for a spell, to give them some privacy. She would tell no one about Ian attending the birth. But thank God he did, for Maggie had needed him. And why should a man not be present for the birth of his own child?

She shook her head. The event was entirely too much for her mind to fathom. She reached behind the counter to where Ian kept brandy for medicinal purposes and poured herself a small amount. It burned down her gullet like fire, but after a few more swallows, she relaxed.

"Have some more, Bethan. You deserve it." Ian's voice carried into the shoppe. Maggie's chuckle and the baby's wail followed, then Ian's soft melody. The babe stopped crying.

"Let's call him Daniel, after your brother."

"Daniel," Ian murmured. "Yes, he would like that. I hesitate to say…" He cleared his throat. "Do you think his head will always be so…misshapen?"

"It's quite normal, did you not know that?"

"No, I didn't. Beautiful boy."

Bethan put down the glass, remembering she still had things to do.

"I'm going to examine you, Maggie."

"I want to move to the divan. My back aches lying

here."

With more confidence than when she'd begun, Bethan checked Maggie and ascertained the bleeding was no more than normal. She had Ian hold the babe while she helped Maggie to the divan, propping her up with pillows. She took young Daniel from Ian and watched as he slowly transferred himself to the chair, and then the couch.

"I'll dish you out some soup, clean up the baby, and make him a posset."

"Give me the babe," Maggie said.

Bethan placed him in the cradle. "Eat first."

Before Maggie could argue, she placed the bowl of stew in her hand.

Ian had pulled himself onto the divan. "Look at my son. He seems to have your calm demeanor, my love." Indeed, the babe gazed at the ceiling with a still alertness.

"You must rest when you can, Maggie. You had a most difficult time."

Maggie looked up. "Yes."

"It was most extraordinary. I felt the Holy Nun's hand guiding me."

Maggie handed her the empty bowl. "I would not have believed it, but she has aided me when I needed it most. The falling sickness I suffered from is one of the most serious conditions a birthing mother can experience. Most women die. Why I didn't I don't understand. You've seen the healing power of Julian of Norwich. She is always there to aid you when you cannot help yourself."

Bethan nodded. "It was a miracle."

Maggie kissed the top of the babe's downy head.

"Yes, but you are also skilled, Bethan. It is an innate, instinctive gift that will only improve with time."

"Thank you for putting your trust in me."

"You are the town's midwife now, for the time being."

Bethan nodded. "I vow to study the book you gave me. There's so much I don't know."

"Being a midwife is a humbling vocation, and there is always something new to learn. Don't fret, Bethan."

"I will always do my utmost," Bethan said.

"Get some rest, Bethan," Ian said. "And thank you."

She handed the babe to Maggie. "I'll fetch you both more ale, and then I'd better get back home."

"Thank you," Maggie said.

"I never imagined I could be this happy," Ian murmured. He uncovered the blanket to admire the ruddy skin and tiny hands and feet. "He is perfect. See how he wriggles his toes? Thank you, Maggie mine."

Maggie kissed him. "You were rather necessary in the making of our boy, husband."

Bethan eased the door closed and met the morning sun with a joy and exhilaration she'd never known. A realization chilled her like a cloud passing over the sun: one minute she could be breathing, and a minute later, her life could be over. If she died today, what would she wish she'd experienced above all else?

Warm brown eyes, and pleasure cascading through her like a waterfall whenever he touched her. What if she died, still yearning? Why could she not have what Maggie and Ian had? So many things seeming impossible before had come to pass; the spirit of the Holy Mother still whispered through her.

What a difference a day could make in a life. She had arrived at Maggie and Ian's unsure of herself, and left with a glow of confidence that almost lifted her off the cobbles.

Chapter Thirty

Lena met her with open arms when she arrived at the inn. "*Liebchen*! Are Maggie and the baby well?"

"A boy, strong and hearty."

"*Gott sie danke*!" Lena clapped her hands. "I will bring a pot of oyster stew to her tonight."

At that moment, all the strain from the long night made Bethan's knees shake.

"*Ach*, sit down. You're shaking." Lena led her over to a chair by the fireplace. "Have you eaten?"

"No."

"I just fried some fish. I'll bring some to you."

"Lena, you needn't wait on me. How is my sister?"

"Elunid is in her room, sewing. She was up before me and seems well enough."

Bethan made to rise. "I should check on her."

"No. You will sit right here and eat. Then you'll nap."

Bethan was too tired to argue.

Lena soon handed her a plate laden with haddock and ale.

"You must care for yourself, Bethan. It's what I'm always telling Maggie. You can't care for others unless you care for yourself."

Bethan nodded, head spinning when she did so. She closed her eyes against the dizziness.

"And there is more than one way of caring. There

is the caring between a man and a woman. Henry, he dotes on you, *Liebchen*. And you care for him."

"How can there be room in my life for love, with all of my concerns?"

"Being a martyr won't keep you warm at night."

"What about Elunid, Lena? Why would he want to take us both on?"

"Love grows, Bethan."

She wanted to believe it.

"And I wouldn't underestimate Henry."

She nodded. "Can you sit with me, Lena?"

"No, I must see to Sabine."

"Is aught amiss?"

"She has a fever and is vomiting."

"Oh no!" She made to rise but plopped down again, overcome with dizziness.

"Now, what have I just been telling you, Bethan? Sit."

"Thank you. The fish is delicious, as always."

"There's more in the kitchen. Eat, then sleep."

Once she'd finished, Bethan leaned her head back and closed her eyes.

A blast of cool air slipped under the cover of her dreamless slumber.

"Da, there she is."

She startled like a baby at a loud noise.

"Aw, George! You woke her up." Henry's deep voice.

She bolted upright and opened her eyes with effort, meeting young George's brown ones. She blinked.

"Ergh."

Henry appeared with a cup of tea in his hand. "Here. Nice and hot." He handed her the cup, took a handkerchief out of his pocket, and wiped the slobber running down one side of her face.

How humiliating. She stared stupidly at him. She'd never noticed he had gold flecks in his brown eyes before.

"I heard about the babe. Well done, Bethan."

Her breath caught in her throat at the pride in his voice.

"I heard it wasn't an easy birth."

She sipped her tea, and felt awareness return. When had he noticed she liked it sweet?

"He's a handsome boy. Like your George."

"How did the baby get here?" George asked.

She opened her mouth, shut it again.

Henry snorted, then coughed to cover it up. He waited, head cocked, eyes brimming with mischief. "Bethan?"

She scowled at Henry. Suddenly the image of his nude body glistening with water came unbidden to her mind. Damn!

"Are you well, Mistress Bethan?" George peered at her. "You're very red."

"Yes, yes. I'm fine. Thank you, George." She glanced at Henry out of the corner of her eye. He looked every bit like a lad who'd snatched a pie from the windowsill.

"How did the baby come?"

"Fathers are very good at answering those questions, George." She smirked at Henry.

"I'd like a little brother, Da." He waited expectantly.

"Uh."

Bethan was enjoying Henry's discomfiture when

George turned toward her.

"You brought a baby for Mistress Maggie. Surely you could bring one for me."

She felt Henry's eyes on her and couldn't look away. "Yes," he murmured. "Surely you could."

The need in Henry's eyes opened a chasm inside her that only he could fill.

While still looking at her, Henry said, "George, go to the kitchen and see if there's anything to eat."

He leaned down and clasped Bethan's hand. "I'm sorry we could not have our picnic last night."

"Oh." She'd forgotten. "I'm sorry too." Why should she bother pretending? Perhaps Lena was right. He certainly looked strong enough to withstand anything, even Elunid's troubles.

"Tell me about what happened last night. Well, not the loathsome details, obviously."

"It was harrowing. Maggie became very ill."

He searched her face, as if he would feel her emotions.

"It was exhilarating. It was exhausting."

"Yet in your sweet face I see strength and vigor."

"I love delivering babies. I never thought I'd have anything in my life besides caring for Elunid."

"Do you have room for me, Bethan?" His voice slid into her and warmed her very core.

"Let me take you on our picnic tonight if you're not too tired." He lifted her hands to his mouth, and rested his lips against them, his breath raising the little hairs on her arm. She gave herself a little shake.

He laughed. "Are you well, Bethan?"

She pulled away and stood up, causing him to step backward and trip over the hearth.

Lena entered, carrying two squalling babies.

Henry grinned. "Here, Lena. I'll take one."

Bethan watched as Lena handed little Josef to Henry.

"I must get cooking." Lena handed Sabine's babe to Bethan.

"Hullo, lad." He jiggled the boy, who quieted and grabbed hold of his curly black hair.

"Oh, ouch." He made a face, causing the babe to stop his crying and chortle.

Bethan stood and reached up to uncurl the baby's fist. No wonder he wanted to grab hold. Henry's hair was so soft and springy, it seemed to have a life of its own. Henry cradled the side of the babe's head and gave him a finger to chew on.

As she watched him, the words came unbidden from her mouth. "How easy it would be for you to marry Lena."

He stood stock still. "Did I hear you correctly?" He paused, then smiled. "I don't want 'easy,' Bethan. I want you." Despite the babe in his arms, he breached the gap and kissed her soundly, the babes squawking between them.

"We will have our midnight picnic."

Henry's promise seemed like a fairy tale as the evening went on. Rum seemed to be the preferred drink, and tempers ran high. Bethan's ears buzzed with the din of shouting and singing.

Reginald and Vicar Andrews shared a table, and what an unlikely pair they were. It seemed they shared a mutual fascination for Sabine, who had rallied round and returned to work, almond-shaped eyes huge in her pale face. The two men looked like a pair of bass with their eyes on the same bait.

There was no time to talk throughout the evening, but as Henry and Bethan crossed paths, he never failed to touch her in some way: the brush of his arm against hers, sending frissons of thrills up her arm, a hand upon her shoulder making her feel safe and calm against the riotous behavior of the crowd. It was like a voice of calm silencing the chaos of the crowd, saying, "I am here." Strength and promise.

She took a moment to check on Elunid, who'd gone to bed. She thought at first she was asleep, but Elunid opened her eyes.

"What's the matter, Elunid?"

"Nothing. I'm resting my eyes."

"You've been working very hard today."

"I hope it's enough."

"You can't go blind trying to sew for them, Elunid."

"Can I not? Would it not prove my dedication to them?"

"No one thanks a martyr, Elunid."

"Easy for you to say, Sister. Now let me rest."

She met Henry on the way out.

"How is she?" He searched her face and gave her arm a reassuring squeeze.

"She's calm, even if she's not quite making sense. I can't ask for more."

He caressed her shoulder. "You've been on your feet for hours, running back and forth between the kitchen and the tables. How is it you manage to look so fresh and lovely?"

She laughed. "I don't know why you feel the need to flatter me so. You needn't. I know I'm big and gawky. My mother told me so, and if your own mother doesn't tell you the truth, who will?"

"I will. I don't want to malign your mother." He caressed her neck, making her lean into it. "But her eyesight must have been very poor."

The rest of the evening disappeared in a flurry of work. Later, they surveyed the clean room, and Bethan sighed.

"Here." He handed her a glass of ale. "This will revive you."

Lena slumped at the table. "*Meine Gott*. What a night. Sabine, dear girl, sit down. Your face is the color of last week's cream."

She could easily go to bed, but the constant touch from Henry throughout the night had bolstered her strength like a good meal. And tempted her to want more.

Young George lay by the fire, sound asleep. Sabine covered him up with a blanket. "Boy worked hard today. He lift heavy things."

Henry walked to the kitchen and returned with a basket. "Bethan, we are going on a picnic."

"It's night," Sabine said. "Picnic?"

"Yes, a meal outside. It's nighttime, but the moon is very bright."

Sabine nodded. "Picnic. Yes."

"Go! I will check on your sister before I go to bed." Lena shooed them toward the door.

Henry fetched Bethan's shawl and wrapped it around her shoulders, his fingers lingering. When he opened the door, a light breeze from the channel kissed her face.

"Fresh air," she exclaimed.

"Yes, and quiet."

He took her arm, tucked it into his side. He wore no waistcoat, yet heat radiated from him.

"You're not cold?"

He laughed. "Oh, I assure you, I'm never cold when you're around."

"What's in the basket?"

"You'll have to wait until we get to our destination."

"You like to keep me in suspense, don't you?"

He nodded. "I'll do what I must to keep you entertained, my dear."

They passed the Landgate, and Bethan stood under it, putting her nose against it and sniffing.

"What on earth are you doing?"

"Old stones have a unique smell. Every time I walk under the Landgate I wonder about all the people who have passed this way. I guess you could say I'm sniffing history. Did you know Queen Elizabeth came to town and passed under this very gate? What was she thinking? Do you suppose she liked the town? What about all the people who accompanied her?"

"You are the most curious person I know." He kissed her.

"Oh!" She put her arms about his neck and kissed him back. "How many people do you suppose have kissed, like this, under the ancient Landgate?"

He leaned his forehead against hers. "Oh Bethan. How you invigorate me."

He put his arm around her, and they walked on the old path. The moon lit the trail in front of them, and cast shadows on the trees standing sentinel on the path.

"Tell me more about Maggie's travails."

"You promise not to laugh at me?"

"Of course not."

"It was a most…spiritual experience."

"How so?"

"After the birth of the babe, Maggie convulsed."

"What causes such a thing?"

"Ill humors and who knows what else? Maggie only said it happens sometimes."

"How frightening it must have been for her."

She stopped. "Please, don't tell anyone. Ian stayed at Maggie's side for the birth, and I'm glad he did, for I don't know if she would have survived otherwise. It *was* frightening."

"I imagine so. You said it was spiritual?"

"In the midst of my fear and distress, a woman's voice, calm, gentle, yet possessed of great might, filled my body."

"How miraculous."

"You don't think I'm crazy like my sister?"

"No. Not at all."

They walked on.

"She told me what to do, laid her hands upon me in blessing. She guided my hand, and a current ran through me and through her. And the convulsions stopped."

"My God."

"Do you believe me?"

"Of course, I do, my love."

She should tell him not to call her that endearment, for she could never be anyone's "love."

But just for tonight, she would pretend. She would grab what warmth and tenderness she could. She would discover what it felt like to be loved by a man like

Henry. Life was too fleeting not to.

He led her onto a narrow path, and the scent of honeysuckle mingled with the fresh salt tang of the ocean.

"I have a special place in mind for our picnic. I've never taken anyone there before. When we first came to town, I was so angry and lonely. I'd come up here and sit, and it would bring me peace." He held the branches for her as they came through an opening to a clear view of the sea below the cliff.

"Oh, it's breathtaking."

He set the basket down, took a blanket out, spread it on the grass. She gazed over the churning sea, at the stars bright in the sky, the moon lighting their picnic place as if just for them.

"Come, Bethan. Let me feed you."

She approached the blanket and sat down.

He took two wine glasses and a bottle out of the basket. He handed her the glasses and opened the bottle, pouring the red wine into the ornate crystal. Then he removed a round of cheese, a loaf of white bread, a jar of blackberry compote. With great aplomb, he set a peach and a dish of liver pâté on the blanket.

"What a feast! I've never seen goblets so fine."

"I've been saving this wine for a special occasion. It's quite old."

"What is this special occasion?"

"You."

Chapter Thirty-One

He kissed her to carry his point home. As if to honor the special night, the wind had let up, and the waves crashed against the cliff, making the ground beneath them tremble.

The moon caught the cut edges of the crystal goblet as she held it, causing it to sparkle like a ruby. "I feel as if I'm in the pages of a fairy tale, among myths and legends."

He needed no myths with her beside him. He broke the bread, not turning his gaze from her, reveling in her sense of wonder. "Are you hungry, Bethan?"

"Yes, I didn't realize how much until now."

He was starved—had been—since he'd held her in his arms, warm and soft, her silken head against his shoulder, his member hard against her soft curves.

Her eyes had turned midnight blue, and she watched with rapt attention as he spread the pâté on the bread and put a dab of blackberry jelly on it.

"Oh! Is that blackberry? I love blackberry."

"I know." There were other things he could think of to put utter delight upon her face. He held the bread to her mouth.

She laughed and took a bite, darting her tongue out to catch a drop. Her eyes grew large. "I never knew such a strange combination could be so good. Salty, sweet..." She licked her lips.

He reached over, and as slowly as he could without dying, kissed her. "More?"

"Yes."

She stared at him with such intensity he thought he'd not be able to take another breath. He fed her, until his fingers touched her lips.

"Your lips are as soft as rose petals," he whispered and kissed her again.

He fixed another piece of bread with a generous dollop of blackberry, fighting to keep his hands from trembling. But he missed, and the jam fell on his white shirt.

He reached for his handkerchief to wipe it off, but she grabbed his hand.

"Let me." Before he could stop her, she lowered her head and gently sucked the blackberry off. His muscles tightened at the feel of her lips and her tongue, and her breasts soft against his lap. If she continued…

He straightened, and as if waking from a dream, she jerked her head up, swallowed hard. He grasped her shoulders, kissed her blackberry-tart lips.

He cleared his throat. "Are you enjoying the wine?" He poured her another glass, handed it to her.

"This must be special wine. I feel as if I'm drinking an entire vineyard in every mouthful."

The wine sparkled like a ruby against her fingers. She took a sip. "And it's sweet, but not overly much." She peered at him from above the glass. "No one's ever taken me on a picnic before, let alone a moonlight picnic."

"I'm glad I could be your first."

"I can't imagine it being any other way." She blushed then, twin spots of cabernet. "This wine must have cost you dearly."

He shrugged. "Yes, but more precious is the memory of the trip to Italy with my brother. Before…"

"How is it you were able to go to Italy? It sounds like something a wealthy lad would do."

He would encourage her curiosity, for it so enlivened her. He merely shrugged and smiled. "How is it you've never been on a picnic?"

"My mother was unwell and fearful, especially after Father died. She was afraid to let us out much. Our sister Polly, who as you know is several years older, had the bulk of caring for us."

"You were like a damsel locked in a tower, waiting to be freed."

She nodded. "Looking out the windows of the lighthouse, I'd see the ships come and go, but never met the people, and always wondered what their life was like. I was always watching…waiting for my life to begin."

She grinned at him, spread her arms out. The moon cast the luster of pearls on her goddess arms, perfectly rounded, long fingers with the power to undo him, the power to give him life.

"But I'm free now, have lived more since I came here than I ever did before." With one hand she removed her kerchief and took the pins from her hair, let the silken curtain fall down her back.

He reached over and ran his fingers through the silken strands. "The moon glints silver on it. So many colors: chestnut, onyx, bits of copper throughout."

She leaned into his hands. "I've not had my hair touched in so long and never by a man."

He was fiercely glad.

She gazed at him. "Thank you for taking me here."

"May I embrace you?" He gestured toward the moon-kissed sea. "There's no one to interrupt us here, and I would take my time with your lips. I've been dreaming about your lips."

He ran a finger lightly against her lower lip, and she grasped his shoulders, kissed him, the kiss of a woman aroused. He wrapped his arms around her slender back and answered her kiss with his own.

"Closer." She moaned against his mouth.

He let his fingers trail down her shoulder blades and up her sides to feel her fine shivering. His thumbs grazed the sides of her breasts, and she gasped. He kissed her until he felt he would burst from the joy of it.

"Bethan, the thought of kissing you has sustained my dreams for weeks. To be in your company, in communion with you now..." He had not thought her passion could be so innocent and instinctive.

She broke away, breathless and windswept.

"Bethan."

She undid her bodice slowly, never removing her gaze from his.

"You..." He should tell her to stop. But how could he not kiss her shoulders, ivory in the moonlight, resolute and delicate? His eyes lingered on the swells of her breasts.

"Love me this night, Henry. I want to feel as others do," she whispered. Her lips glistened with their kiss.

She cast the bodice aside, removed her skirt, and in the silver light her nipples strained against the linen shift. She looked like a statue of a moon goddess, tall and benevolent, a giver of life and light.

Like the sea reaches for the moon, he lifted his

hands and trailed his fingers down the marble smoothness of her shoulders. He kissed her, and she moaned in his mouth. He let his fingers trail to the hollow of her breasts, and one by one, he held them in his palm.

She pressed her body into him. "Please," she whispered.

He took his hands away. "No, Bethan."

Anger, need, and vulnerability flitted across her face like scudding clouds. "So little I can call my own. Could I not have this night, for myself and for you?"

"I would not use you so." He hadn't meant to say it so harshly.

"I would use *you*." She lowered her eyes, the temptress, gazed at him from under her lashes. "I would use you, have wanted to since I saw you by the pond."

No, not this way. "Marry me, Bethan."

She untied her shift, let it fall to reveal her breasts, perfect and silken, an offering. "Give me this night. Love me."

He would use her desire for the sake of their forever. "Marry me, Bethan."

He drew near and lay her down, held one silken breast, took her tender nipple in his mouth. "Will you, my love?"

He paid tribute to her other breast with mouth and tongue, and her back arched. He lifted his head, held his breath at the magnificence of her body. "Will you marry me, Bethan?"

She moaned as he kissed the tender skin of her belly.

"Yes." She lifted her hips. "Yes."

"Soon?"

"I will marry you, my Henry. Just don't stop."

****

"Yes." She would agree to the impossible, to have his touch upon her skin. The rest could wait until tomorrow.

He trailed his kisses along her neck, kissed each breast, then her mouth again. The low rumble of his voice reverberated through her, sent a jolt to her center. "You are magnificent. How I've longed to do just this…" He sat back on his haunches, powerful and wild. His dark gaze swept over her, as if she were a holy relic. "I would worship you every night like this, Bethan. As your husband, for eternity."

She sat up and unfastened his shirt, running her hands over the muscled plains of his chest and the tight, quivering stomach. His labored breath made the fine hair on her neck rise. All the while her gaze met his.

"I love you, Bethan."

She kissed the hollow of his throat. "I'd not thought it possible to love anyone like this. To want anyone." She grasped him by the shoulders, felt the strength and restrained power in the broad muscles. "Love me, Henry. Show me how to love you."

He trembled as she slowly removed his shirt. She paused to breathe in the scent of cedar and the mystery of him. She lowered her eyes to his breeches, where the outline of his manhood strained against the cloth.

"Do not think me wanton. Think me selfish, for I've never wanted anything as much as I want you."

She untied his breeches, slid her hands over the thick length of him through the cloth.

"Bethan," he moaned.

She slid his breeches down over his muscled

thighs, took them off. The wind blew again, a cold blast from the channel, but he was solid, wide-shouldered, and quite still, his hair untied and blowing about his face.

She grasped his manhood with both hands. "It's so smooth and warm."

"Yes, you must hold onto something in this wind," he rasped.

She laughed, but her breath caught in her throat. "Am I hurting you?"

"God, no." He very gently removed her hands, placed them on his shoulders. "I have imagined this many times, and never has it ended too soon. So as much as I want your touch on me, now is not the time."

She shivered, as a gust of wind assaulted her hot skin.

He had misinterpreted her shivering for fear. "Bethan, are you sure? We don't have to do this."

"You look very much as if you do."

He smiled, kissed her. "It doesn't matter what I want. What do you want?"

"Cover me, Henry."

He closed the gap between them, lowered her to the blanket.

She gasped when skin met skin. He was burning, the rough hairs of his chest like kindling to her fire. He braced his hands on the outside of her body and kissed her again, lowered his head to her breast, and she buried her fingers in his hair.

He trailed his lips down her neck, kissed one nipple, traced it with his tongue, wrapped his lips around it and drew from it, as the moon draws the ocean waves.

Her body rose to meet him. Could he not get closer?

He slid his hand down her belly, down to her womanhood, waited. "Yes?"

She nodded.

He ran his palm across it, lightly.

She gasped.

He paused. "Do you want me to stop? Because I will. No matter how hard, er, difficult it would be. If you have changed your mind."

"No."

He sighed. "Thank God."

He kneeled over her, shielding her from the wind, and parted the folds of her womanhood with fingers gentle and sure. Heat pulsed in her center, through every limb, and all that existed was the pull of her body toward his.

"More," she gasped, and pulled him on top of her, reached down to grasp his member. She guided it to her, lifting her hips. He held himself there, and entered her, his heat sliding slowly into her yearning center. When she heard him moan, she lifted her hips. A piercing pain, there and gone, as he thrust. Then, motionless, he held himself there, and she could feel every inch of him.

He withdrew and thrust again, and a warm tingle swept over her body. She pulsed around him, cried out, as the stars whirled around her.

"Bethan."

Another jolt of pleasure shot through her like a comet at the sound of his voice, and his love crashed over her.

She wrapped her arms around him as he collapsed

on top of her, exulting in the solid feel of him. Chills of pleasure echoed through her body.

He lifted his head, smoothed her hair with one hand. "Thank you."

She laughed, making him bounce against her. "There's no need to thank me. It's I should thank you, for making my first time…there are no words for how I feel."

He started to roll off her.

"No, stay. I love the feel of you on top of me."

"I didn't hurt you?"

She laughed again and kissed him, whispered against his mouth. "You made me feel part of the air, the water, the sky. Do I sound silly?"

"I felt the same."

He rolled off and grabbed a linen napkin, knelt in front of her. "Let me care for you."

Her eyes drank in his dark strength, as if he'd emerged from the earth like primitive man. He gently dabbed her womanhood, and she gasped.

"Am I hurting you?"

"Not at all. It's pleasurable. Is it always like this the first time?"

He eyed her with a fierce pride. "No, not necessarily." He resumed his duties, a smile lifting the corners of his mouth.

"How many times can it happen?"

His voice sounded choked. "As many times as you want."

"Really? How marvelous!" She laughed in sheer delight, then stopped short. Was she wanton? Would he mind?

She might as well ask. For she would make this a

night she'd remember in the lonely days to come. "Would you…"

He grinned, full out then, his white teeth in contrast against the dark stubble of his beard. "Nothing would give me more joy. There are many ways to bring you to your pleasure, other places I would kiss you. May I?"

He sounded every bit like a boy asking for another helping of pudding.

She caught her breath, and by way of saying yes, kissed him.

When she cried out a short time later, he covered her up with the cloak, and leaned on his side, watching her face. "Just rest, my love. Enjoy the afterglow."

"What a wonderful way of putting it. But I'd like to learn to give you pleasure, Henry."

"You're not too tired?" His eyes were shiny as new toffee, and as sweet.

And then he taught her, with gentle guidance and great joy, how to make a man feel alive. What she wouldn't give to be his willing student always.

Before long, dawn lit up the edges of the sky, and after they packed up their supplies, they stood together, breathing in the crisp salt air of the sea.

"I promise you this will not be our last midnight picnic, Bethan."

If only it could be.

Chapter Thirty-Two

She was so busy watching the rising light play on Henry's face, she barely noticed the stares of the early rising townspeople as they made their way into town.

Her body glowed every time he met her gaze, the sun turning his eyes topaz. What would it be like to greet every morning with the joy of him?

The afterglow of their passion was soon doused when they returned to the Siren Inn. Henry and Bethan entered to find it unnaturally quiet, except for the sound of Sabine retching in the corner.

"Oh, my poor dear!" Bethan rushed over, helped her up.

Sabine held a rag to her mouth.

"Go to bed, Sabine. I'll take care of you."

She gulped and nodded.

Just then, Lena stumbled into the room from her private quarters.

"Lena, are you ill?"

"No, I'm fine. I must feed the babe." And without another word, she turned around and disappeared.

Henry stood above a sleeping George. "I'll lend you a hand." He peered at the big kettle over the fire. "The kettle's full."

"Thank you."

"No thanks needed. I am at your service. I'll go into the kitchen and see about making a broth." As

Henry passed by, he touched her cheek. "Bethan, love. We will face life's troubles together, thee and me."

She tried to smile, but the weight of what must be done had already doused the glow from her.

He kissed her lips lightly. "And we will share the joys as well."

"We've no time to talk about it right now, when there's so much to be done."

And suddenly the evening in the moonlight seemed only a fairy tale.

"I must check on Elunid."

****

Bethan opened the door to Elunid's room.

"Elunid?"

The bed was empty, bedclothes strewn on the floor.

"Where are you?"

The ewer and basin lay in pieces on the floor, the armoire had been emptied, clothes littering the room.

In the far corner, Elunid crouched naked in the fetal position. Her anguished keening raised the hairs on Bethan's spine, and as she rushed toward her sister, terror crashed into her like a rogue wave. She steeled herself against it and gathered Elunid in her arms.

Elunid stiffened and struggled, slapping Bethan across the face. Bethan struggled to hold her, arms burning with the effort. Elunid's head hit her chin, and the sour scent of fear radiated from her. Bethan sought to find the words; their old language could sometimes break through the chaos of her mind.

"*Sligh-manon, meecheh.*" She crooned over and over, rocking her back and forth, panic smoldering in her chest. She willed her mind to reach her, at the same time afraid to fall into the abyss, into her sister's agony.

"Ellie, please. I'm here. Ellie."

She didn't know how long they remained there, rocking. Her voice ached from crooning; she pressed her lips against her sister's forehead, tasted her sweat borne of fear. A nameless malignant presence hovered over them.

She managed to lift Elunid up and carry her to bed. She had stopped her keening but hissed like a snake with each breath. Now she was laid out, Bethan's gorge rose at shallow scratches covering Elunid's body. She grabbed a night rail on the floor and wiped the blood off as best she could. Had she done this to herself? She'd never harmed herself before.

She fought against the horror clawing its way up her throat. *Breathe, Bethan. Think. You must help her.* There was only one thing to do: tend to her wounds and dose her up with medicine.

"Sweet Sister." She covered her shivering body with a sheet and reached for the ointment in her apron. She rubbed the ointment over the scratches. Perhaps the scent of the marigolds would soothe her. She found her night rail and dressed her, covered her with blankets, stroked her forehead, willing her to close her eyes. What horrible things had she seen to make her do this?

She dared not leave her, but she must put the medicine in something. Ah. A half empty teacup sat on the bedside table. Ian had said this batch was stronger, but she would double it. She kneeled on the bed and lifted Elunid into a sitting position. It was like moving a wooden doll.

"Sweeting, you must take this." She pried her mouth open, poured the scant liquid into her, and closed it, pinching her nostrils shut.

Elunid sputtered and choked, but the liquid stayed down. Bethan waited. She curled up beside her and put her arms around her cold, still form. She fell asleep.

She awoke, disoriented and aching in every limb, but Elunid lay sprawled in bed, asleep.

She rose and pulled the covers up to her chin. The medicine worked. For now. And that's all she dared ask for, wasn't it? She set the room to rights again, picking up the broken shards of pottery, shattered like Elunid's mind.

****

This one, he liked to whisper praise in one ear when she sewed a Beauty Stitch, and sew her finger to the cloth when her hands faltered. Marred the needlework with the blood. How was she to please them if he profaned her work? She'd had to start all over.

The second one had come when she was young still, to sever her from Sister. Hissing hate, praising hate. If she didn't listen, he put boils on the young girl's face, lifted the skirts of old women. Screamed obscenities now, for she had been too close to *Chwaer* of late. He loomed over her, the buzzing of flies around his head, red eyes seeing into the shame boiling inside of her, red eyes bidding her to answer his call. Threatened to ugly her *Chwaer* with sin, make her his. No. *I am already ugly with sin. Take me.* She let his darkness swallow her.

****

She returned to the main room to the sight of Henry at a table, holding little Josef, who stared at him, and with impressive strength, pulled his hair out of his tie. Despite her fatigue, the cozy domesticity of the scene did much to strengthen Bethan. She fetched them all a mug of ale and sat down with Henry.

"Bethan, are you ill?"

"No, I'm fine. It's Elunid. But she's sleeping now."

"Why did you not fetch me? I could have helped."

"I couldn't leave her." And besides, this was her battle to fight.

"I thought perhaps you'd fallen asleep. I'm a little tired myself, but not sorry." He grinned, then paled when she didn't smile, but merely kissed the top of her head. "Look at poor yon Vicar."

Vicar Andrews sat morosely viewing a plate of fried kippers. "Mistress Bethan, may I be of use? Mistress Sabine, I could serve her some soup, perhaps minister to her."

"I bet you could." Henry concealed his smirk behind the baby's head.

She poked him in the arm.

"Thank you, Vicar. But I fear it would be most improper of you to do so."

"And you very well know that," Henry said.

Vicar blushed. "Will Mistress Sabine be okay? She is very delicate."

Sabine, despite her slight figure and quiet nature, was one of the strongest women Bethan knew. Everyone knew the vicar carried a torch for her.

Young Johnny burst into the inn. "Mistress Bethan. I've been sent to fetch Mr. Henry and you to the apothecary's house."

"Are Mistress Maggie and the baby okay?" She reached for her cloak.

"Yes, they're well. But it's something else. I was told not to say." The boy waited, and Henry threw him a coin.

Bethan and Henry exchanged a worried glance.

"They would not summon us unless it was important." Henry turned to George, who made himself useful by dandling Sabine's baby on his knee. She giggled as he sang "Banbury Cross" to her, which made him laugh as well.

"It's a big responsibility I'm putting on your shoulders. You are the man of this establishment, and must see to everyone's needs as best you can. Check on Sabine, and put the babes in their cradles if need be. If anyone needs to be waited on, fetch their ale and use what's in the kitchen."

"Vicar can collect the coins and help with the babies. Give the girl to him," Bethan said.

"Aye." Eyes wide, George handed the baby to Vicar.

"Aren't you just one of God's sweet creatures," Vicar crooned, a look of mild panic on his face.

"She said you must hurry." The boy still stood at the doorway.

Henry came and took her arm. "We'd best be on our way."

When they got to the shoppe, Martha, the baker's wife stood weeping over her daughter, Isadora.

Isadora lay on the divan, crying in great, ragged sobs.

"My poor Isadora! What's happened to you?" Her mother, Martha embraced her.

"Don't touch me." She had a blackened eye and a ragged cut upon her cheek. Her bodice was ripped at the neck and hanging from her in tatters.

Ian approached. "Isadora, this will help calm you."

She cringed. "No."

"They found her staggering through the Landgate," Maggie whispered. "She was insensible."

Isadora hid her face in her hands, and rocked back and forth.

Martha wrung her hands. "Who would do this you? You are ruined, Isadora, ruined!"

"Martha," Maggie said, in a tone commanding authority. "Go to your cottage and fetch her some food. I'm sure she's hungry. And she'll need to bathe in the tub."

Martha nodded and swept out the door.

Ian took the crying babe from the cradle and followed Henry into the shoppe, closing the curtain at the parlor's entrance. "Let's leave the women alone to minister to Isadora. I sent my messenger boy to contact the constable."

"Now then." Maggie handed the tea to Bethan. "Martha needed something to do and will be the calmer for it when she returns, I hope. Isadora may not have wanted to say anything in front of her mother. Perhaps she will talk now."

Bethan nodded. "Isadora, drink this. It will ease your pain. Here, I'll help you. There now."

"Someone has molested her," Maggie whispered. "There is blood on her... I need to examine her when the herbs take effect, see if there's anything I can do for her." She shook her head.

"I'm soiled," Isadora cried.

Bethan kept her demeanor calm and comforting, but inside she fought a rising panic. She took the cup from her and soaked a cloth in a basin of warm rose water. "Here, let me clean your face. It will feel good."

After a while, Isadora threw off the blanket and straightened in the chair. She took a long, shuddering breath and sobbed again, tears pooling in the pockmarks on her cheek. "I thought he was different. He said I was beautiful. He said I was a rare jewel, one to be treasured."

She laughed then, an odd choked sound, raising the hairs on Bethan's neck. "He promised to take me away to exciting new places and give me children who would love me."

"Who did, Isadora?"

"Freddy. I thought he loved me."

"You thought he loved you," Bethan echoed.

Isadora laid a hand on her womanhood, covered her breasts with her other arm. "But he didn't, he hurt me. He ruined me." And she wrapped her arms around herself, rocking back and forth. "I'm a fool."

"Can you tell us anything else, so we can bring this man to justice?" Maggie gingerly sat down beside her.

"No, I cannot talk about it. No."

"Isadora, you must understand. This not your fault. You mustn't blame yourself," Bethan said.

"I will not hurt you, I promise. But I need to look at you, see how best to help you," Maggie said.

"Don't be afraid."

Isadora nodded.

Maggie hurriedly examined her. "As hard as it is to believe this now, your wounds will heal. I see no permanent damage."

At least physically. "Isadora," Bethan said. "I must return to the Siren Inn, but I will come and visit you tomorrow, if you'll permit."

Isadora nodded.

Without warning, a jolting pain slammed into Bethan's back. She stifled a cry of pain. Then, just as quickly, it subsided. Had the trials of the day, the excitement and distress finally caught up with her? No time for this, not when she had so many people to care for. At least Elunid was asleep, and likely would be for a while.

She said her goodbyes and stepped into the shoppe, where Ian puttered around, the babe in his arms.

"I have some herbs to ease Sabine's nausea."

"Ian," Bethan said. "It seems as though your mixture might be of help to Elunid. She's sleeping soundly after…well, she's sleeping soundly."

"Excellent." His hearty exclamation had startled the babe, who wailed with impressive volume.

"We must be getting back," Henry said. "I've left George in charge."

"Good lad," Ian said absentmindedly, his head bent toward his boy. "I've a song for you, wee one."

Bethan grinned as they walked out, then sobered at the thought of poor Isadora.

Henry took her arm as they walked back to the Siren Inn, a brisk wind from the channel hastening their journey. "The poor girl."

"Her life will never be the same," Bethan murmured.

"She could be happy again."

"How can you be so optimistic?" Bethan turned to him. "No one will ever have her, ruined as she is."

"She may find a good man who will love her despite her past."

"Not likely."

He reached up to smooth her forehead. "Never

doubt the love of a good man."

She quickened her pace. "There are many who need our care right now. We can't think of ourselves."

They entered the inn to find George sound asleep by the fire.

"Poor lad," Bethan said.

Upon hearing her voice, he jumped, then swayed. "Oh Da! I'm sorry. I tended to Sabine as you asked, and the babes are asleep, and I was so tired."

"It's okay, George. Go back to sleep. You did well. Have you seen Lena?"

"No, I thought she was asleep. Oh, I don't feel so well." He held his stomach and vomited.

Henry rushed to him. "George!"

Just then, a pair of dusty travelers walked in.

"Welcome," Bethan said. "Can I fetch you some ale straightaway?"

They nodded and sat down by the window.

"I must check on Elunid," Bethan said.

She hurried to the private quarters and into her twin's room. The bed lay empty, her embroidery strewn in pieces on the floor. "Elunid!"

She searched the room, the armoire, the corners, under the bed. She stood in the middle of the room, gasping. *Breathe, Bethan.* She could be anywhere, in a corner of the inn somewhere, caught up in her visions. She opened her senses, reached out for her.

No. She may have just gone to find more thread. But her embroidery—she never would have thrown it on the floor. Her cloak was gone, though. The jolting pain in her back returned, and she gasped as the babble of tormented souls assaulted her ears. She must find her. *Chwaer.*

She searched the remaining rooms to no avail and found Lena in the ale room, holding her stomach.

"Elunid is gone."

"What's this?" Henry burst into the kitchen. "Are you sure?"

"Yes, I can feel her. She needs me."

"I'll help you search."

They searched the inn, to no avail.

"I must stay with George," Henry said. "But if you wait, I'll set him aright, then help you."

"No, I must go now."

She set off for the docks first, but no one had seen her.

"We must search the caves. Pray God she hasn't gone down there."

Some boys played on the beach.

"Lads." She motioned for them over. "There's coin in it for you if you'll search the caves for a woman who looks like me."

"Aye. Let's go."

"If you find her, one of you come and fetch us. I'll be at the apothecary shoppe."

"If she's there, we'll find her."

Mayhap Elunid had gone to seek help from Ian. She hurried over.

Ian was in his wheelchair, readying himself to go out, his face grim. "I was just coming to fetch you. Elunid is gone?"

"How did you know?"

"Go talk to Isadora. She…"

Bethan rushed into the parlor, followed by Ian. "Isadora, do you know where my sister is?"

Isadora burst into tears, crying in great gasps. "I'm

sorry. I never meant for this to happen."

"What are you talking about?" Bethan sat down beside her and rubbed her back.

"I just wanted Freddy to love me." She grimaced. "And now your sister..."

"What are you saying?"

"He said he was only going to scare her. For talking about the wool they were smuggling. He said I would be doing the town a service, if I brought her to him, so they could talk to her."

"They?"

"The Parson too. Freddy said he wasn't going to hurt her."

Unease prickled down her spine. "Where is she?"

As if she didn't hear her, Isadora continued. "Charlotte and I snuck in and lured her to the Landgate, pretending to be her friend. I told her I had some special thread that had been blessed by the angels."

Bethan removed her hand from her back.

"How could I be so cruel? And now anything could have happened to her, and I am ruined."

"Stupid girl!" Bethan clenched her fists to keep from slapping her.

Maggie sat in the rocking chair, feeding the babe. "Isadora. Tell us what happened so we can find Elunid."

"We've been putting ideas in her head, Charlotte and I, for sport. I thought what harm could it do. She's touched anyway." She glanced at Bethan, cringing at the look on her face.

"We snuck her out and led her to the Landgate. Freddy was there, and he took me into the woods, said he must ask me an important question." She gulped.

"Charlotte said she would tend to Elunid."

A fine trembling coursed through Isadora. She moaned and rubbed her face, hard. "He had his way with me, hurt me. Said if I loved him, I would submit to him."

Bethan fought her aversion toward the girl and grasped her hand, saw the skin in her fingernails. She was a foolish girl but hadn't deserved to pay for her foolishness at such a price.

"He led me out of the woods, said he'd return for me. Then the Parson came with the gypsy wagon. When Elunid saw him, she began to scream. She fought like a scalded cat, knocked a tooth out of the parson, gave Freddy a black eye. Maybe if I'd fought like that…"

"No, Isadora," Maggie said. "It's not your fault."

"They finally got her in the wagon, and the Parson said, "Damn it! No one will buy this bitch. We'll take her to where she belongs."

"Where were they taking her?"

"I don't know! Oh God. What have I done?"

Ian grew still. "They must have taken her to Bedlam."

Bethan grew cold, her vision blurring. Her wrists burned with sharp, cold metal.

"I must go."

She made haste back to the inn, with the echo of her sister's anguish in her head.

Chapter Thirty-Three

Henry was standing over George's reclining form when suddenly Bethan burst into the inn. He rushed over to her.

"I must get her out. Now. I'll find a horse and…"

"Bethan. Where is she?" Henry grasped her arm.

"They took her to Bedlam hospital."

"I can help."

She pulled her arm away. "You don't understand. This is my fault. If I'd been tending to my sister like I should have, instead of enjoying the pleasures of your flesh…"

"This is not your fault. I am your future husband. I'll help you."

"You know it could never be."

He tamped down his anger. Arguing with her would not help her now.

"Listen to me, Bethan. We must have a plan. You can't just walk in there and get her out."

"I must go now."

He put his hands on her shoulders. "You must trust me. I can get her out. But I must leave now, and there is no time to explain. Wait here for me. Do you hear me? I have a way to get her out."

She had the look of her sister about her right now: confused, altered. "You don't understand. I can feel her pain, her fear and despair." Her shoulders heaved as she gasped for breath.

"Please, my love." He held her face in his hands. "Listen to me. Trust me. I will get her out."

She nodded.

"But I must leave now. Do you understand, Bethan?"

He kissed her. "Will you take care of George for me while I'm gone?" Mayhap it would keep her from doing anything foolish.

She nodded again.

He would ride to his solicitor's in London now, use his influence. He would do whatever it took to get Elunid released from Bedlam, even use the influence of his family.

****

"Bethan, don't worry. Henry will get your sister out." Lena stopped for a moment to reassure her.

But how could she do nothing while her sister suffered? For she could feel the cold bite of the cuffs around her wrists, the rank, fetid smell of the place, the echoes of terror in the hoarse voices of souls who'd screamed until they could scream no more. No. She must go. *You can trust no one else but yourself. Hasn't it always been so?*

It didn't take long before she was on the road. The moon had been so kind last night. It still shone bright, but tonight the glow cast shadows onto the path before her. She took the horse from the post outside the inn. Who it belonged to, she didn't know or care. Every thought, every emotion had blown out of her like a leaf in cold winter winds. Saddle the horse, steal the clothes. She could look like a man: breeches, waistcoat, slouch hat.

She urged the horse on and out the Landgate. The few people she encountered on the road backed away at the fierce look on her face, and as the trip wore on, road dirt and sweat disguised the details of her face. She rode into the night, Elunid's moans of anguish rising above the relentless rhythm of the horse's hooves on the dirt- packed road.

In hours, minutes, or days, she knew not, the fresh pre-dawn air of the country gave way to the stench of London. She stopped in a thicket of trees to adjust her clothing, made sure her hair was tucked into her hat. Her limbs shook with fatigue.

She'd followed her sister here, now what was she going to do? She had the herbs in her pocket, the ones Ian had given her for Elunid. She would use it on the keepers as well.

As she stood out of view, she heard the sound of another horse.

Reginald appeared, wind-blown and cursing.

"What are you doing here?"

"Lena sent me to keep you safe." He got off the horse. "She figured out what you were doing fast enough."

Why would Lena send shallow Reginald to help her?

"Bethan, what are you doing? You must wait for Henry." He handed her a flask. "Drink this. Bethan, what in hell were you thinking, coming here alone?" He scowled. "And you ride like the devil himself."

She drank deeply and shoved the flask back.

"Even as we're enjoying Lena's good ale, Elunid is suffering."

"You're very beautiful, but foolish, Bethan."

"Do you love anyone more than you love yourself, Reggie?"

He winced. "Touché."

"I would give my life for my sister."

"You don't need to if you wait for Henry."

"I can trust no one but myself. It has always been so."

"God, woman! I see there's no convincing you."

"We must hurry. The sun will soon be up."

"Do you have a plan, or are we just going to waltz in there and use our good looks as a weapon?"

"We'll drug the keepers, then we'll just…take her out." She put her foot in the stirrup.

"What? Bethan." He grabbed hold of her.

"Get out of my way!" She whipped around and slammed her fist into his jaw. "Help me or leave."

"Shit! Bethan, I must warn you, despite my charming demeanor, I'm not a brave man."

Chwaer, help me.

"We must act. I know—you will pose as her fiancée. I will be her brother."

He rubbed his jaw. "You have an arm for the part. And a preternaturally low voice."

"Do you have money?"

"Yes, Lena supplied me."

"I have some as well. Also some gin, which we'll put the herbs in. We'll bribe them to get in, and bribe them to get out. We'll say she's a wild one in bed, like no one else."

"Good God, Bethan! I'm shocked a woman of your gentle upbringing would think of such a thing."

So was she. "Let's go. Now."

Before long, they reached the imposing structure of

Bedlam hospital. A guard slumped against the wall, dressed in blue livery smeared with filth. Before she had time to be afraid, Bethan swaggered up to him. Reggie hummed his appreciation for her demeanor. She'd seen enough men swagger at the inn.

The keeper scowled toothlessly, an upturned jug by his side. Bethan swallowed her revulsion at the gin fumes blowing from his mouth.

"Need to see my sister," Bethan said.

"Your sister, eh?" He leered.

She showed him the flask of gin and the money. "Yes, ass. She's tall like me. Her fiancé here can't do without her. She's a hellcat in bed."

"She nearly killed us all. We could barely get near her."

Good. "I know how to calm her down."

Reginald bowed. "I will compensate you well. You see, I must have her. I'll return her to you, and no one needs to know."

"Is that so?"

"Here's what we do: you let him see his fiancée, you get some of this." She flashed the bag of coins. "And when he returns her, you get more."

He licked his lips. "Why her?"

"She's a hellion in bed, but she's too crazy to keep."

"Good luck to you. No one'll even touch her."

Bethan breathed a sigh of relief.

"She's possessed, stronger than an ox."

"Let's get her. Now."

The keeper blinked his bloodshot eyes. "Follow me then, fool." He stumbled down the fetid corridor, falling against the cages. The poor souls behind them cried in a cacophony of misery and entreaties. She tried to hold her breath against the stench of urine and feces.

They followed him all the way to the end of the corridor. The keeper stopped at a cell, turned to fumble with the lock, and while his back was turned, she assessed the situation. She was taller by several inches and had the advantage of being sober and desperate. She knew how to fight. He was strong in the arms, muscular, but she was quicker.

He glanced back at her. "Here's your fiancée. Enjoy." He chuckled, wheezed, and coughed. "Now where's my gin?"

She thrust the bottle at him. He snatched it, put it to his lips, and gulped, his throat exposed. She drove her fist into it with all her might, battered his balls with a well-aimed kick. He fell, and she struck him across the face with the jug, pouring the contents over him. No movement.

"Jesus, Bethan." Reggie snatched the keys from the man's hands.

Elunid lay on the floor in a threadbare shift. Her face was gray in the dim light, her lips pressed together, eyes wide and unfocused.

Reggie fumbled with the locks on her manacles, while Bethan watched the corridor. No movement from the keeper. Reggie picked Elunid off the floor.

Bethan embraced her stiff, cold body. "Elunid. You are safe."

Elunid grew limp. "*Chwaer.*"

Thank God. They hurried down the corridor, Reggie struggling to hold the shivering form. And finally, they reached the entrance and out into the brightness of day. As they moved away from the building and toward their waiting horses at the inn, Elunid let out an ear-piercing, staccato scream.

Two men in blue livery pissed on the wall of the inn. They turned their heads at the sound.

"What in hell is… I know her. The tall one."

"Hey there. Why do you have her?"

The other guard nudged his partner. "Come on, man. We're not on duty yet. We got time for another drink."

"If we bring her back, we'll get a reward."

The two men rounded on Bethan and Reginald, grabbed hold of Elunid, who screamed again.

"Get away from her," Bethan screamed.

The keeper stumbled out of the doors of Bedlam. "There's the one who escaped."

Bethan knew what she must do.

"Reggie, go. Take her to Ian."

"What?"

She approached the men, screaming in words only her sister would understand.

"No, Bethan!"

"What's this?" The two men turned toward her.

She fell upon them, aiming for their faces, scratching, arms flailing.

Reggie seemed frozen, damn him! "Go, Reggie."

"That's her," the keeper screamed.

As they carried her into Bedlam, Bethan watched Reginald and Elunid disappear.

Chapter Thirty-Four

He'd done what he had to do to help Bethan's sister. And he could do more now, more than he could have done as a night soil man, without family or connections. He left the solicitor's office with the funds he needed to free Elunid, but it came with a price. Had his family changed? Would they receive George, love him as he deserved to be loved? He risked his boy's happiness for her. He could only hope it wasn't in vain.

He rounded a narrow alleyway, nearly colliding with Reginald, who struggled to hold a body in his arms with one hand, the reins in the other.

Reginald stopped.

"You have Elunid?"

"I'm sorry, Henry."

"What's happened?"

"Bethan…it happened so fast."

"Tell me, damn you!"

"Lena sent me to keep Bethan safe while you did what you needed to do. We, well, *she* got Elunid out. But then something happened, and Bethan took Elunid's place."

"She took her sister's place in Bedlam?"

"Yes."

"My God." His vision blurred with anger. "Damn it, Reggie! How did you let this happen?"

He fought for control. The damn, foolish, brave

woman. She'd sacrificed her life for her sister. He should have known she'd do such a thing.

"Wait here. I'll hire a carriage so you can get her to Ian."

This was accomplished in short order and Henry helped Reginald put Elunid in the carriage.

"I'm sorry I failed you, Henry. I wasn't built for bravery."

"Just get Bethan's sister home safely."

Reginald nodded. "I swear it."

He would need it. Pray God nothing had happened to Bethan yet.

He arrived shortly at Bedlam's gates. Henry was finely dressed, as befit someone of his station. He tried his best to keep the anger from his face.

At the office by the entrance, the man in charge looked up from his desk. "Yes, sir."

Henry bowed. "My fiancée needs to be released immediately. I'm willing to compensate you for her safe and prompt release." He showed the man the gold coins. His eyes grew wide, then resumed their normal size in the blink of an eye.

"I see no impediment to your desire, sir…"

"Lord Henry James Stephens, Viscount of Barton. At your service."

"What is the lady's name?"

"Bethan Owen."

"Oh, dear." He eyed Henry warily.

"What is it? What have you done to her?"

"I'm afraid I can't let you take her, no matter how beneficial it may be for myself, a man with so many children to feed."

"Why not?" He advanced upon the man.

"You see, I cannot. She aided another prisoner in escaping and assaulted three men, one she almost killed."

"You will let her out." He grabbed the man by the throat.

The man backed up. "Guard!"

Through the haze of anger, he heard feet stomping, and a burly, foul-smelling giant of a man loomed over him.

"As much as I'd like to let her go, I cannot. I'd lose my job."

"I'd pay you enough to live your life out well, and the lout here, too."

"No. My father and my grandfather both worked here. It's a matter of pride. Now I will ask you to leave, and you will leave peacefully."

Henry fought the urge to pound his fists into both of them. The stench of misery on the giant's clothing nearly choked him.

"I see."

He would find another way in. Pray God he could save her in time.

****

They had shaved her head as soon as they'd thrown her in her sister's cell. The blade rasped against her skull, her dark hair falling on her lap, and the men picked it up, held it to their noses.

"She's fine, isn't she? So soft, these locks." They rubbed them on their face, their arms, their bulging genitals. "What's she got below?"

The nicks on her scalp burned, and tiny rivulets of blood ran down her head. She couldn't wipe it away, for her wrists were manacled. She covered her ears against the endless din, like surf in a storm. But it wasn't surf, it was suffering: fear, sweat, shit, chaos. Shouts, singing, begging, howls, and entreaties washing over her like the tide. She couldn't make out the words, but she heard them all. How long would it be before *she* would cry out so?

She tried to sing to drown it out, but every song she knew disappeared, and the stench of vomit and feces filled her nostrils. Her stomach twisted. She shivered. No wonder Elunid had done so. It was dank and cold as the bottom of the sea.

But Elunid was free. And hadn't she said many times she would change places with her sister? Henry said he'd get Elunid free, but so too had others made promises they couldn't keep. For he had never arrived, had he? Since when had there been anyone to depend on besides herself?

She'd fought them off, so far. Mostly. She could rub the one spot within reach where they'd pinched her. The one she'd hit over the head threatened he'd return after his duties, as he rubbed her shorn hair over his bulging cock.

She eyed the bowl of slop they'd brought her. She should eat, for how could she fight if she didn't eat, and she would fight her hardest. She held the bowl to her mouth, gagged at the rotten stench, closed her eyes against the bits of moving objects in the weak broth. She must eat.

Eventually, she finished the contents of the bowl and kept it down; she had succeeded in that. At least she was alone in her cell; who knew for how long? At least she had the memory of Henry's touch upon her skin, his deep voice making her feel safe and beloved.

And a memory was all it would ever be.

One thing reigned above all else. Elunid was safe.

Chapter Thirty-Five

He slipped into the inn next to the hospital. He had to think. He would get her out of Bedlam, and soon, but brute force wasn't going to work. They were on high alert. He scanned the dismal environs of the inn: low ceilings, worn chairs, worn people. Anything of any value had been stripped from the place long ago.

A brawny, whiskered man stood over him, "What will you be wanting, Toff?"

Nothing but suffering seeped from these walls. The occupants were either workers, or family members seeking courage before visiting their kin in hell. Then there were those who hungered for the base and depraved, leaving a filthy scum upon his skin.

A pair of them huddled in the corner, snickering at what the crazed fools would do for a sip of gin, a bite of bread. Didn't matter did they stink or not, the lunatics would do anything.

He shut his mind to it. Reggie had told him where she would likely be. Was there a back way in? Who enters the place, and no one takes notice of them doing so?

All of a sudden, it was so obvious he wanted to slap himself for not thinking of it. Who did people like to pretend didn't exist?

He'd smelled the stench of cesspits needing to be emptied. Time for the local night soil man to appear.

He left the inn to find the night man who serviced the place. It didn't take long to ask around, not with a handful of gold coins. When he found him, the man was more than willing to comply, and no wonder. He wouldn't make that much in a year.

After donning borrowed work clothes, Henry drove the wagon to the spot the night soil man had indicated and set about emptying out the cesspits there. He encountered a worker who'd just stepped outside the door of the hospital and approached him.

"What ye doing in here, night man? Kind of early, ain't it? Sun's just gone down."

"Here to do a bit of extra cleaning, empty some buckets as a service to these poor souls who abide here. Free of charge." He reached into his pocket, handed him a flask. "It's me own recipe. Rough, but slides down the throat just the same. I'll be out of here before ye know it." He'd dosed the whisky with some of Ian's herbs.

"Aye, then. Come in. I'll sit out here a bit, wait for ye."

Henry slipped into the dark corridor. She was here somewhere.

****

She cowered in the corner now, the floor wet with urine. He'd chained her feet, too. She fought with her head, butting, biting him. Almost fainted as fatigue set in, but kept moving. At least he was drunk. After a while, he gave up, slapped her, and no doubt moved on to someone who'd not have the strength to fight him. But he'd return.

If only she had some ale or wine to wash the taste of him from her mouth. The wine she'd shared with

Henry, on the moonlit night—she would drink the whole bottle if she had it. She closed her eyes, took herself to a time of gentleness and peace. If she had but one more chance to make a vow with him, a vow for eternity.

The next time, there were two of them.

"Ye're a sad sot, if ye can't do what needs to be done with this 'un."

"She's the strongest lass I've ever tried to swive."

"How bad can she be?" This one was sober and well-muscled. His eyes crawled over her. He reached down and fondled her breasts. "You're beautiful, lass. Do what we ask, and we'll see to it you get fed. We'll take care of you, we will."

She'd try a different tactic. If she was unshackled, she could do more damage. Mayhap she could escape? She looked the strong one up and down. "How can I do you properly if I'm chained?"

The two men eyed each other.

"There's two of us, and one of her. What harm could she do?"

She'd do what she had to do.

They unshackled her, ran their hands down her arms, legs. The strong one grabbed her breasts roughly, his stringy hair sliding on her face, rancid breath turning her stomach.

She forced herself to take in air. How could she fight two of them?

She smiled sweetly, silent and compliant.

"I'm first. Watch me lad, and see how it's done."

He laid his knife down and kissed her. The ridge of his erection rubbed against her stomach. She bit his lip, hard, blood filling her mouth. She trod on his instep, and when he yelled and backed away, kicked him in the knee. He threw her to the ground, and as her head hit the wall, the world went gray.

****

He heard her scream, ran down the corridor, and nearly rammed into the man standing at the cell door. He set upon him with his fists, grabbing him by the neck and banging his head against the ground.

A figure lay on top of Bethan, was lifting her shift, his breeches about his ankles. Henry pulled him off her and slammed him against the wall. She lay unmoving. They'd hacked her hair off. What else had they done to her?

The man he'd thrown off Bethan came toward him, fists at the ready. He hit Henry in the stomach, and Henry tackled him to the floor. They wrestled, and Henry felt the sharp sting of a knife against his back.

He tried to wrest it away, and pain sliced into his thigh as the knife went in. He wrapped his arms around the man's neck and squeezed until the man lay still. He tossed him aside and ran to Bethan.

He picked her up, ran down the corridor and out to the wagon.

"Henry?"

"My love. You are safe now."

She stared at him, eyes wild.

"You're free. We're going home."

Comprehension lit her face. "How?"

He smiled. "However I could."

"Elunid?" Her voice was hoarse. So like her to think of her sister first.

"I'm sure Reginald got her home, and by now she is in Ian's fine care."

"I should go to her."

"You need taking care of, Bethan."

She nodded, then was silent for a while, shivering. She sniffed.

"A night soil wagon. Not mine."

"What?"

"I'll explain later. We must leave."

He set her in the seat and covered her with his cloak. "We must go, and quickly. Will you be all right?"

She nodded. "My God. You came for me." She began to shake uncontrollably.

He got in, urged the horse on, and they made their way out of town. Once away, he grabbed his shirt from earlier and took the knife out of his thigh, grunting with the effort.

"You're hurt." Her voice was weak but steady.

"It's nothing." He tied the shirt around the wound to slow the bleeding.

"We must wash it soon, so it won't fester," she croaked.

So like her to be more concerned about him than herself. He handed her a jug of water, and she held some in her mouth and spat it out.

"What are you doing, love?"

"Nothing. Just…getting the taste of them out."

He struggled to keep the rage from his voice. "Did they…assault you?"

"No. You arrived in time. Just."

As the chaos of London gave way to the peace of the countryside, he began to breathe normally. The impact of what had occurred hit him now: he had killed a man and would do it again, for her.

They stopped at an inn he knew well between King's Harbour and London. He picked her up and carried her through the door.

"Henry, my good man!" The rotund innkeeper rushed to his side. "What have we here?"

"My fiancée is ill. She needs a hot bath, food and wine, and would your kind wife possibly loan her a dress?"

His eyebrows rose. "Of course, all those things."

They were soon settled in a small, but serviceable room. Everything Henry had requested had been done in short order, and they were left alone with a tray of cheese, bread, and wine.

She sat huddled in his cloak, not eating. "I'm filthy, and I reek."

"You must be starving, though. Eat first before you take your bath."

"No. And I'm ugly now." She touched her head, wincing when she touched the nicks.

"No, Bethan. You are rare and exquisite."

"I must wash the stench of Bedlam off me." She walked over to the tub, took off her shift.

He helped her into the tub.

She sighed as she submerged, sunk under the water. When she emerged, she sounded a bit more like herself. "Oh, it feels wonderful. I never thought I would be warm again."

He kneeled at the edge of the tub. "Lie back, Bethan. I'll wash you."

She complied and closed her eyes. "Scrub hard, Henry."

She said it with such vehemence he had to ask her again. "Bethan, did they…did they hurt you?"

She shuddered. "They…touched me, pinched me a bit. I fought them off, but they would have overpowered me eventually. I got them to take my shackles off and thought to play along, and thus I'd be more able to fight."

He rubbed the cloth with violet-scented soap and started with her face, then skimmed the cloth over the bruises on her shoulders and breasts, gritting his teeth in anger. He took great care with her body, humming under his breath.

"Clever girl. Lean forward, so I can get your back." They'd scratched her where they'd pawed her, the bastards. He had no regrets for what he did, would do it again if need be.

"The water smells so good," she murmured. "Violets. No one's washed me since childhood."

"I'll do it every night when we're married, if you wish."

"I'll not argue with you anymore. I will marry you." She grabbed hold of him and kissed him, getting his shirt all wet.

He helped her from the tub and gently dried her off. "Your wrists are raw from the manacles. Ian will have some ointment for you."

He helped her with her night rail and put her to bed. He piled the pillows behind her and served her a plate of cheese and bread and a goblet of wine.

"Henry, you're hurt."

He looked down. "It's fine."

"No, it needs tending to. It's bleeding. At least let me look at it, in case it needs stitches. I won't rest until you do."

He sighed and removed his breeches.

"Here. Sit upon the bed. Let me see it."

Her touch upon his skin was blessed agony. So was the whisky she poured over the wound, without giving him a chance to say yea or nay.

"It needed to be cleansed thoroughly," she said, after the fact.

He handed her the plate of food. "Eat." He cleared his throat. "Remember when I left after Elunid disappeared and told you there was something I must do? I need to tell you something."

****

She nodded.

He met her gaze. "I came to King's Harbour from northern England. When my wife died and George grew to the age of three or so, it became obvious he was not quite like the other children. He didn't walk until he was two, said not a word until he was almost four, but he could sing—no words—just his little voice, echoing on the walls of the nursery."

She nodded and watched his profile in the moonlight, the proud span of his shoulders.

His voice thrummed with anger. "My family would not accept George. They wanted me to give him up so I could start over, as if he was a botched pie to be thrown away."

"Oh. How could they?"

His eyes grew dark, and he had a pleading look on his face. "I must tell you something. I am not who I say I am."

"What are you then, Henry?"

"I'm a viscount."

Without thought, she laughed. "A viscount? Why do you say it the same way you might say, 'I'm a

257

leper'?" She laughed.

He'd turned a brick red. "I met with my solicitor, to send word to my family to make amends, so I might use my title to get Elunid out. They had been pleading with me to reunite with them for some time."

"How is it you became a night soil man, Henry?"

"When my family rejected my boy, I vowed to make another life for us. Then the final straw came when I found George in the nursery, crying and injured. He was all of four years old. His cousins had set upon him, hit him, and derided him. When I approached my mother and father, they made light of it, said it didn't matter, for he was too stupid to feel it."

"Oh, I see." She grasped his hand.

"So I left, and we settled in King's Harbour, where the people accepted us. Being a night soil man is a job George will be able to do when I pass on."

All of the pieces of the puzzle began to fit into place: Henry's manners, his knowledge of Shakespeare, his skill with language and music.

He eyed her, a grin playing on his face. "Will you still find me as fascinating, now you've solved my mystery? Now that you know I'm Lord Henry James Stephens, Viscount of Barton?"

The enormity of it hit her then. "This will take some getting used to, Henry."

"I'm the same man I've always been."

She grinned. "So to save George, you were a viscount who became a night soil man, and then you became a viscount who disguised himself as a night soil man to save me."

An odd expression passed over his face. "Yes, I suppose so."

She embraced him. "You have saved us all, and a lifetime won't be long enough to solve the mystery of you. Climb into bed with me, beloved. Hold me, and comfort me with your strength."

"You must be exhausted, Bethan. We have a lifetime to love each other."

"I can't sleep just yet. Too much has happened. Kiss me, Henry."

He enveloped her in his arms and kissed the top of her head. "Are you sure?"

"I would start our new life properly." She kissed him, and lifted his shirt over his head. "Come here."

He lay beside her and held her against him. She kissed him again, enjoying the roughness of his beard. He removed her shift, and her center melted at the feel of his heat against her skin, hard muscle against soft flesh. She twined her fingers in his hair, trailed them down the back of his neck, kissed the hollow of his throat, the broad chest. She enjoyed the salty taste of him, the coarse hairs tickling her nose, and his groan when she sampled his nipple.

His manhood lay pulsing against her stomach. She rose above him to slide against his ridge, her soft, slick, center sending thrills of pleasure through her. He ran his palms over her shoulders, down to her breasts, cupped them, took one in his mouth.

"Henry."

She grasped his member and slid the smooth hot length of him into her with agonizing slowness, so she could feel her center pulsing around him. She drew him deeper into her, flung her head back as he bucked under her, pleasure cascading through her in waves. He cried out, pumped his essence into her, carrying her weightless on the tide.

"I feel as if we're at sea, floating on the water, entwined. And nothing can sink us; we can withstand any storm, as long as we're together," she said.

"Together we are stronger than anything that may befall us."

"I will be your strength, and you will be mine."

He kissed her. "Whatever the morning brings, we will face it together, you and I."

Epilogue

Lena had outdone herself at the wedding feast. The Siren Inn burst with happy guests, and rang with music from Ian, and the Wandering Wastrels—minus Charlotte, who had disappeared. Reggie didn't seem to care a whit.

Henry, the night soil man and Bethan sat at the head of a table groaning with Lena's best victuals. Bethan glowed in the peacock dress and wore an indigo blue bonnet on her head.

Young George sat next to Henry in a new blue suit, talking with a mouth full of trifle. "Mistress Bethan, er Mother." He grinned. "I've a mother now! And a grandmother as well."

On Bethan's other side, Henry's mother, a petite, silver-haired lady, smiled. "Yes, you do indeed."

Elunid, also dressed in peacock attire, sat next to Widow Jenkins, embroidery in hand.

Widow Jenkins said, "I'll teach ye a stitch hasn't been done for years, if my warty old hands can do it."

Elunid handed her the cloth.

"Not now, lack-a-wit! It's your sister's wedding supper."

Elunid's eyes grew round, then she met Bethan's gaze and smiled.

Henry's father, a stocky man with white above his temples, leaned over to talk to Henry. "So your mind is made up to stay in King's Harbour?"

"Yes, Father, as I've told you many times over. We will spend some time in the summer on the estate, so George can get to know his cousins."

He nodded. "I can see why you love this town. Everyone is quite congenial."

"And those who aren't don't last long," Reggie said. "They took Freddy to London, but they've not found the Parson yet."

"Let's not talk of them," Lena said. "Isn't it time for the blessed couple to kiss again?" Her cheeks were rosy with ale, and her eyes seemed just a little bluer when she glanced at Reggie.

"Aye," cackled Widow Jenkins. "Have you had your peas, Henry? For when you bed a giantess, you must be armed with all the help you can get."

Bethan blushed. Everyone knew peas were known to give a man vigor in bed. Henry couldn't possibly have more vigor than he already had. The touch of his leg against hers made her feel as if the fabric would burst into flames.

Henry rose and took her hand to stand at his side. He raised his glass to her. "To my Bethan, courageous, strong, and beloved. May we face whatever life brings us joined together, buoyed with hope, laughter, and love."

"Hear, hear."

They kissed, the promise of the future like music on their lips.

A word about the author…

Jennifer Taylor spent her childhood running wild on an Idaho mountainside. Although she's lived across the U.S., she's still an Idahoan at heart and a notorious potato pusher. She has a degree in Human Services and has been a roofer, a computer data entry operator, a stay-at-home mom, and a professional singer and dancer.

Music plays a big part in her historical romance series, and she can often be heard singing at her desk…unless she's writing a midwifery scene, where screaming is more appropriate.

Jennifer feverishly lobbies for the return of breeches and would love to see her husband of thirty-four years in a pair.

She lives in rural Florida with her husband and an entitled Great Dane.

Jennifer can be reached at:
jenntaylor888@gmail.com.
www.jennifertaylorwrites.com
https://www.facebook.com/jenniferrtaylorwrites/
@jenntaylor888